WAS MAN DOOMED

FOREVER TO SENDING

MESSAGES BY SMOKE

SIGNALS?

The Earth, after the atomic holocaust, had reverted to a strange kind of barbarism where men could build space ships but could not communicate except by the most primitive means.

So it was a sickening shock to Lord Clane Linn when he captured one of the alien invader's space ships and discovered that their central headquarters in another galaxy was sending them messages and getting answers.

There was no possibility of sneak attack against such an enemy. With this weapon alone the aliens could win the war—unless Earthmen discovered the secret and how to use it . . . before the next assault.

THE WIZARD OF LINN

A. E. van Vogt

MB

A MACFADDEN-BARTELL BOOK

THIS IS THE COMPLETE TEXT
OF THE ORIGINAL EDITION

A MACFADDEN BOOK......1968

MACFADDEN BOOKS are published by
Macfadden-Bartell Corporation
A subsidiary of Bartell Media Corporation
205 East 42nd Street, New York, New York 10017

THE
WIZARD
OF LINN

I

The "child of the gods" had made progress. Born a despised mutation into the ruling family of the half-barbarous, decadent Linnan empire about 12,000 A.D., he had grown up almost unnoticed by those in the family and government who schemed endlessly for power. Contemptuously relegated to the temples for training, he learned the inner meaning of matter from a few wise men who had guessed the secret behind the atom gods. By the time his potential enemies realized that he might be dangerous to their plans, he was too powerful to be destroyed.

He explored the gigantic pits where the atom gods were believed to dwell, and learned that they were remnants of destroyed cities. From these husks of what had once been megalopolitan centers, he gathered odds and ends of machinery and weapons, including a sphere of energy that absorbed or disintegrated all energy and matter it touched, except—this was a guess on Clane's part, based on the fact that so tremendous a weapon had been unable to defend the vanished civilization—"protected" matter. The sphere reacted to the thought of the person who controlled it.

His discoveries explained many things. They explained the half-mythical stories about a long-dead wonderful civilization that had apparently existed some thousands of years before. They gave a clearer picture of how a bow and arrow culture could exist side by side with simple-type spaceships that any skillful metal worker could build, and they offered a partial explanation of the so-called "god" metals which powered the ships. But the mystery of the forgotten disaster remained unexplained.

And then Czinczar and his barbarian hordes from Jupiter's moon, Europa, invaded Linn. He brought with him the dead *body of a large, nonhuman creature. Czinczar believed that long ago other such beings had come from the stars and obliterated man's civilization. And though his own attack against the Linnan Empire failed, his statesmanlike attitude toward the welfare of the human race enabled him to convince Clane that the presence of one monster in the solar system implied that another invasion was imminent. Clane who had come across vague references to a Riss enemy in ancient books, was impressed by the barbarian's sincerity. But he rejected Czinczar's demand that he take control of the Linnan Empire. There were too many complications.*

There was, for instance, the fact that the new Lord Adviser, Lord Jerrin, was his brother.

In the deceptive darkness of space, the alien ship moved with only an occasional glint of reflected sunlight to show its presence. It paused for many months to study the moons of Jupiter, and the Riss-creatures aboard neither concealed the presence of their ship, nor made a particular display of it or of themselves.

A score of times, Riss exploring parties ran into human beings. Their policy on such occasions was invariable. They killed every human who saw them. Once, on remote Titan, the hilly nature of the terrain with its innumerable caves enabled a man to evade the net they spread for him. That night, after he had had ample time to reach the nearest village, an atomic bomb engulfed the entire area.

For what it was worth, the policy paid off. Despite the casual way their ship flew over towns and villages, only the vaguest reports of the presence of a big ship were spread. And for long no one suspected that the ship was not occupied by human beings.

Their precautions could not alter the natural order of life and death. Some hours out of Titan, a Riss workman who was repairing a minor break in an instrument on the outer skin of the spaceship, was struck by a meteor. By an immense coincidence, the flying object was moving in the same direction as the ship and at approximately the same speed. The workman was killed by the blow, and swept out into space. On Europa, the largest moon, a Riss one-man exploring craft made its automatic return to the mother ship but without its pilot aboard. Its speedometer registered more than a thousand miles of flight, and those who tried to follow its curving back trail found themselves over mountains so precipitous that the search was swiftly abandoned.

Surprisingly, both bodies were found, the former by meteor miners from Europa, the latter by troops engaged in grueling maneuvers preliminary to Czinczar's invasion of Earth. Both monstrosities were brought to the leader; and, putting together various reports he had heard, he made an unusually accurate guess as to the origin of the strange beings.

His attack on Earth took place a few months later while the alien ship was still in the vicinity of Europa. And his defeat at the hands of Lord Clane Linn followed. The machine from the stars continued its unhurried voyage of exploration. It arrived on Mars less than a month after Lord Jerrin and his army embarked for Earth, and another month went by before its presence was reported to the Linnan military governor on Mars.

A descendant of the great Raheinl, he was a proud young man, who dismissed the first account as a tale of simple imagination, all too common in these regions where education had fallen a victim of protracted wars. But when the second report came in from another section, it struck him that this might be the Martian version of the barbarian invasion. He acted swiftly and decisively.

Police spaceships and patrol craft scoured the atmosphere. And, since the alien made no effort to avoid being seen, contact was established almost immediately. Two of the police craft were destroyed by great flares of energy. The other ships, observing the catastrophe from a distance, withdrew hastily.

If the Riss noticed that they were now in a more highly mechanized part of the solar system, they did not by their actions let it disturb them. If they guessed that in these regions their action meant war, they seemed equally unaware of that.

The governor dispatched a warning to Earth, and then set about organizing his forces. For two weeks his patrol craft did nothing but watch, and the picture that came through was very satisfactory to the grim young man. The enemy, it appeared, was sending out exploring parties in small ships. It was these, on the fifteenth day, that the human-manned ships attacked in swarms.

The technique of assault had been very carefully worked out. In every case an attempt was made to ram the Riss craft. Four of the attacks were successful. The smashed "lift" boats glittered in the dull afternoon light as they fell to the flat earth below. Swiftly, spaceships darted down, drew the fallen machines aboard, and hastily took off for widely separated landing fields.

It was a major victory, greater even than was immediately suspected. The enemy reacted the following morning. The city of Gadre blew up in a colossal explosion that sent a mushroom of smoke billowing up to obscure the atmosphere for a hundred miles.

The ferocity of the counterattack ended the war on Mars. The alien was left strictly alone thereafter. The youthful Raheinl, stunned by the violence of the response, ordered the evacuation of the larger cities, and dispatched another of a long series of warning reports to Earth. He also sent along for examination the two largest and least damaged of the enemy small craft which he had captured.

It was about a month later that he ceased to receive reports of the ship's presence inside the Martian atmosphere. He concluded that it had departed for Earth, and made out his final report on that basis. He was relieved.

The problem would now be faced by those who were in the best possible position to know if it could be handled at all.

Jerrin put down the first report from Mars as his wife Lilidel entered the room. He rose to his feet, and gravely assisted her and the babe-in-arms she carried—their seventh child—to a chair. Then, uneasily, he returned to his own chair. He had an idea that he was going to hear more about a certain person.

Lilidel began at once. And, as he had expected, it *was* about his brother, Clane. He listened politely, with a sense of dissatisfaction in her, a feeling of exasperation that came to him whenever she tried to influence his judgment for emotional reasons. When she had gone on for several minutes, he interposed gently:

"My dear, if Clane had wanted to seize control, he had two whole months between the end of the barbarian war and my return."

She waited respectfully while he spoke. Lilidel—he had to

10

confess it—was a remarkable wife. Dutiful, good, gracious, discreet, and with an unblemished past, she was, as she had pointed out many times, a model among the women of noble birth.

Jerrin could not help wondering at times what it was about her that annoyed him. It made him unhappy that he had to have thoughts like that. Because, considered in individual segments, her character was perfect. And yet, the woman-as-a-whole irritated him at times to the point of distraction. Once more, he spoke:

"We have to recognize that Clane conducted the barbarian invasion campaign with remarkable skill. I still don't quite see how it was done."

He realized immediately that he had said the wrong thing. It was a mistake, according to Lilidel, to be too generous with appreciation for the merits of other men. Clane had only performed his duty. There was no reason why he should not retreat now into private life, and restrict his ambition for the good of the family and of the state.

Jerrin listened unhappily. He was seriously dissatisfied with the way he had acted towards his brother's victory. At the very least, a Triumph should have been offered Clane. And yet, his advisers in the Patronate had persuaded him that such recognition would be highly dangerous.

When he spoke again, his reply seemed to be a direct answer to Lilidel. Actually, it was partly a defensive reaction to all the people who had held down his natural impulse to give credit where it was due. He said:

"My dear, if some of the things I've heard about Clane are true, then he could seize control of the government at any time. And I should like to point out one more thing: The idea that the Lord Advisership is now a rightful property of my branch of the family is an illusion. We may hold it, but power slips from a person's grasp even as he thinks he has it firmly gripped. I have here"—he picked up the report from Mars —"a most disturbing message from General Raheinl—"

He was not allowed to change the subject as easily as that. It seemed that if he did not have any ambition for himself, at least he could think of his own offspring. It appeared that it was up to him to insure that his eldest son was confirmed in the succession. Young Calaj was now seventeen years of age, and the plan for him should be made clear at an early date. Jerrin cut her off at last.

"I've been intending to tell you. I have to make a tour of inspection in the provinces, and I am scheduled to leave this afternoon. We'd better postpone this discussion till I return."

Lilidel put in a final word on the subject of how fortunate he was to have a wife who accepted his ever more frequent absences with a heavy but understanding heart.

II

SOMEBODY said, "Look!"

There was so much amazement and wonder in the word that Lord Jerrin whirled involuntarily. All around him, men were craning their necks, staring up at the sky.

He turned his gaze to follow that collective stare. And he felt a flame-like shock. The ship up there was enormous beyond all his previous experience. He guessed, from his detailed knowledge of the limitations of spaceship construction on Earth, that it was not of the solar system. His mind flashed back to the messages that had come from his military governor on Mars. For a moment then a feeling of imminent disaster seized him.

His courage flooded back with a rush. He estimated that the stranger was a third of a mile in length. His sharp eyes picked out, and noted for future reference, details of construction dissimilar to anything he had ever seen before. As he watched, the great machine floated by silently. It seemed to be about three miles above the ground, and its speed could not have been very great, because after a minute it was still visible in the distance. It disappeared finally beyond the mists of the eastern horizon.

Before it was out of sight, Jerrin was giving his orders. He had still to receive the message about the destruction of the

Martian city Gadre, but he was more cautious than Raheinl had been. The fleet of spaceships and smaller craft which he sent after the stranger had strict orders to keep at a distance.

The preliminary defensive measures taken, Lord Jerrin returned to the City of Linn, and settled down to await reports. By morning, half a dozen messages had arrived, but they added nothing of importance to what he had personally observed. What did count was the arrival about noon of a letter from Lord Clane.

Your Excellency:

I earnestly urge that you order the evacuation from the large cities of all forces and equipment necessary to the defense of the realm.

It is vital that this ship from another sun be destroyed. There is some reason to believe that those aboard are descendants of the same beings who destroyed the legendary civilization of Earth. Riss they were called.

I request that there be a meeting between us as soon as possible. I have a number of valuable suggestions to make concerning the tactics to be employed against the enemy.

Clane

Jerrin read the note several times, and tried to picture the details of the evacuation that his brother was recommending. Considered in its practical details, the enterprise seemed so vast that he put the letter aside angrily. Later he bethought himself, and sent a reply.

Most Excellent Brother:

All necessary and practicable precautions are being taken. I shall be most happy to have a visit from you at any time.

Jerrin,
Lord Adviser of Linn

When that had been sent off, he wondered for the first time how Clane had learned so quickly of the interstellar ship. It seemed far-fetched that he also could have seen it personally. The incident was merely one more confirmation of

13

his suspicion that there were supporters of Clane in every branch of the service including, apparently, his own staff.

By evening, when the reports about the ship were coming in steadily, the bitterness of his feeling against his mutation brother yielded to the need for a careful study of the mounting pile of evidence.

Now, the alien ship was crossing the ocean. Then it was over the mountains. Next, it stopped for an hour above the city of Goram. A hundred small craft emerged from it, and spent the daylight hours exploring the nearby hills.

In spite of Jerrin's orders that none of the visitor's "lift" boats be interfered with, two incidents occurred. They took place at widely separated points, but were similar in outcome. Both resulted from Earth patrol boats venturing within a mile of one of the small enemy vessels.

Observers reported flashes of blue fire. The Earth craft burst into flame and crashed, killing their occupants.

The news, when it reached him, shook Jerrin. But it confirmed him in a plan that had been growing on him. He had been waiting to hear from Mars the outcome of Raheinl's plan. (He took it for granted that the ship which had come to Earth was the same one that had been on Mars. And that it had merely made the journey from the fourth planet to the third one more swiftly than the spaceship which undoubtedly was bringing the report of the Martian governor.) But now it seemed to him the answer was clear.

The alien had come from another star. Soon, it would go back home. Therefore, since those aboard were making no attempt to communicate with him, they should be allowed to carry on as they pleased. Meanwhile, the Linnan fleet would strengthen its defenses, and be ready for a crisis. When he communicated these instructions to his chief of staff, the officer stroked his mustache, and said finally, "What do you mean—strengthen our defenses? In what way? Have more spears and arrows manufactured?"

Jerrin hesitated. Put in that way, his plan sounded blurred. He said at last. "Be alert. Be ready for sacrifices."

He didn't know what he meant by that, either.

The second day went by while his sense of inadequacy grew. The following morning the officer in charge of the men

14

and women watching Lord Clane and his chief supporters reported that the mutation was moving all his equipment out of his residence in the city of Linn.

Jerrin considered that in a gathering anger. It was exactly the kind of incident that could start a panic, if it became known. He was still seething when a second note arrived from his brother.

Dear Jerrin:
    I have received the news of the Martian disaster, and I urge you to order the evacuation of Linn and other cities.
    I tell you, sir, this ship must be destroyed before it leaves Earth.

Clane

It was a sharp letter. Its curtness brought the color flooding to Jerrin's lean, tanned cheeks. And for more than a minute the tone, and not the contents, absorbed his full attention. Then he thought, "Martian disaster!"

Holding himself calm, he sent a courier to the field where the official ships from Mars always landed. The courier returned empty-handed.

"No ship has arrived from Mars for more than a week, your excellency."

Jerrin paced the floor of the palace reception room. He was amazed, and concerned to realize that he believed that Clane had received information which the government did not have. He recognized that the mutation had revealed a personal secret in letting him know by this indirect method that he had a faster means of communication with the planets. The willingness to let that secret out seemed significant now.

And yet, he could not make up his mind to accept all the implications in good faith.

He was still worrying about it when Lilidel came in. As usual, she brought one of the children with her.

Jerrin studied her absently as she talked. She was no longer the great beauty he had married, though her remarkably even features remained almost unchanged from the day he had first met her.

Not her face, but her body showed the marks of the years

that had gone by, and the children she had borne. Jerrin was not unreasonably critical. He only wished his wife's character had altered as little as her body. He said presently, patiently, "I want to make one thing clear. A man who cannot protect the empire cannot hold his office. I suggest that you cease worrying about the succession of our Calaj, and seriously consider the desperate position we are in as a result of the presence of this strange ship."

Quickly, he told her of the messages he had received from Clane. When he had finished, the woman was pale.

"This is what I feared," she said in a tensed voice. "I knew he had a scheme afoot."

The egocentricity of the remark startled him. He pointed out that Clane could hardly be considered responsible for the appearance of the ship. Lilidel brushed the explanation aside.

"What reason he uses doesn't matter," she said impatiently. "When a man has a purpose, any reason is good."

She was going on in the same vein when Jerrin cut her off. "Are you insane?" he said violently. "Let me inform you madam, that I will not tolerate such nonsense in my presence. If you wish to chatter about Clane's conspiracies against the state, please don't do it to me." His anger aroused by her illogicalness, he forgot for the moment his own suspicions of Clane.

Lilidel stared at him with hurt eyes. "You've never talked to me like this before," she sniffled. She clutched the little girl tightly against her, as if to protect herself from further thrusts.

The action also served to call attention to the presence of the child. There was a pattern to the movement that abruptly pulled Jerrin back along the years, to all the other occasions when she had brought one of their children whenever she came to him with a complaint or a request. *Or a request.* The shock of the thought that came was terrific. He had always been proud of the fact that Lilidel, unlike the scheming consorts of rulers of other days, had never used her relationship with him for private purposes.

Now, he had a flashing picture of the *thousands* of times she had come to him to forward the interest of some individual. She had suggested appointments to positions of varying importance, all the way up to governorships. In her quiet

16

way she had promoted a fantastic number of decrees, orders, and laws, only a fraction of which could possibly have originated in her own mind.

He saw her, suddenly, as the spokesman for a group that had been ruling the provinces he commanded by taking advantage of his preoccupation with military affairs. Through him they had set up a vast organization subservient to their interests. And it was they who wanted to turn him against Clane.

The extent of the betrayal sobered him. It was hard to believe that Lilidel could be aware of the implications of what she had done and was doing. It was easier to believe that her character, too, had been analyzed by clever men, and that she was being used. Unquestionably, however, she must be playing the game consciously as far as she understood it. He did not doubt that she loved her children.

The problem was too great to be acted on immediately. Jerrin said quietly, "Please leave me. I have no desire to talk to you harshly. You caught me at a bad moment."

When she had gone, he stood for a long time undecided, his mind again on Clane's message. At last he thought, *The truth is, I have no solution to the problem of the invading ship. It's time to find out if Clane has.*

His message to his brother was brief and to the point: "Let us meet. Name date, place and conditions."

Clane's reply was, "Will you order the evacuation of all large cities immediately? And then will you come if I send a ship for you?"

"Yes," Jerrin answered back.

17

III

THERE WAS no sign of Clane when the Lord Adviser's party arrived at the spaceship. Jerrin accepted the implications of that with a grim smile, but there were murmurs of annoyance from his staff. The tension ended as an officer in general's uniform came hurrying down the gangplank. He came up quickly, saluted, and stood at attention, waiting for permission to speak. Jerrin gave it.

The man said quickly, apologetically, "Your excellency, Lord Clane sends his sincere regrets that he was unable to complete certain preliminaries. We are to pick him up at his estate, and he will wait upon you the moment he comes aboard."

Jerrin was mollified. He was no stickler for rules, but he did not have to be told that people who deliberately broke them were expressing unspoken purposes and thoughts, which, on the government level, could mean open rebellion. He was glad that Clane had chosen this way to express his purposes. He was fulfilling the minimum of amenities.

Jerrin was not so indelicate as to inquire the nature of the "preliminaries" that had caused the delay. He took it for granted that they existed only in the imagination.

From the porthole of his apartment, a few minutes later, he watched the land recede below, and it was then that his first alarm came, the first realization that perhaps he had been hasty in risking himself aboard this ship without a large guardian fleet. It seemed hard to believe that his brother would risk a major civil war, and yet such things had happened before.

He could not bring himself to admit openly that he might have walked into a trap, so he did not inform the officers of his party of his suspicions.

18

He began to feel better when the ship started its descent towards Clane's estate landing field. Later, as he watched his brother coming across the field, the anxiety faded even more. He grew curious as he saw the men behind Clane were carrying an elongated, troughlike metal object. There was something in the trough that shone, and it seemed to be moving back and forth in a very slow fashion. It was out of his line of vision before he could decide what it was. It looked like a glass ball.

In a short time the ship was in the air again, and presently an officer arrived with Clane's request for an audience. Jerrin granted the request at once. He was puzzled. Just where was this ship heading?

He had been sitting down; but as Clane entered he rose to his feet. The apartment was ideally constructed for a man of rank to receive homage from lesser mortals. From the anteroom, where the entrance was, three steps led up to the larger reception room beyond. At the top of these steps, as if it was a throne dais, Jerrin waited. With narrowed eyes and pursed lips, he watched his brother come toward him.

He had noticed from the porthole that Clane, as usual, wore temple clothing. Now, he had a moment to observe the effect in greater detail. Even in those spare surroundings, he looked drab and unassuming. In that room, with its dozen staff officers in their blue and silver uniforms, he seemed so terribly out of place that, suddenly, the older man could not believe that here was a threat to his own position.

The rigid hostility went out of Jerrin's body. A wave of pity and understanding swept over him. He knew only too well how carefully that clothing covered the other's mutated shoulders and arms and chest.

I remember, he thought, *when I was one of a gang of kids that used to strip him and jeer at him.*

That was long ago now, more than twenty years. But the memory brought a feeling of guilt. His uncertainty ended. With an impulsive friendliness, he strode down the steps and put his great, strong arms around Clane's slim body.

"Dear brother," he said, "I am glad to see you."

He stepped back after a moment, feeling much better, less cynical, and very much more convinced that this delicate brother of his would never compete with him for power. He spoke again, "May I inquire where we are heading?"

Clane smiled. His face was fuller than it had been the last time Jerrin had seen him. Some of the angelic womanlike quality of it was yielding to a firmer, more masculine appearance. Even the smile was assured, but just for a moment it gave him the appearance of being beautiful rather than handsome. He was thirty-three years old, but there was still no sign that he had ever shaved.

He said now, "According to my latest reports, the invader is at present 'lying to' over a chain of mountains about a hundred miles from here. I want you to witness an attack I am planning to make against the ship."

It took all the rest of the journey for the full import of that to penetrate.

At no time did Jerrin clearly realize what was happening. He stood on the ground, and watched Clane examine the enemy ship, which was about three miles distant, a shape in the mist. Clane came over to him finally, and said in a troubled voice, "Our problem is the possibility of failure."

Jerrin said nothing.

Clane continued, "If my use of the Temple metals fails to destroy the ship, then they may take counter action."

The reference to the god metals irritated Jerrin. His own feeling about the Temples, and of the religion they taught, was from the viewpoint of a soldier. The ideas involved were useful in promoting discipline among the rank and file. He had no sense of cynicism about it. He had never given thought to religion of itself. Now, he felt a kind of pressure on him. He could not escape the conviction that Clane and the others took it for granted that there was something in the religion. He had heard vague accounts of Clane's activities in the past, but in his austere and active existence, with each day devoted to an immense total of administrative tasks, there had never been time to consider the obscure tales of magic that occasionally came his way. He felt uneasy now, for he regarded these things as of a kind with other superstitions that he had heard.

Apparently, he was about to be given an exhibition of these hitherto concealed powers, and he felt disturbed. *I never should,* he thought, *have allowed myself to become involved with these metaphysicians.*

He waited unhappily.

Clane was eying him thoughtfully. "I want you to witness this," he said. "Because on the basis of it, I hope to have your support of a major attack."

Jerrin said quickly, "You expect this attack to fail?"

Clane nodded. "I have no weapons better than those that were available during the olden Age. And if the best weapons of that great scientific era were unable to stave off the destruction that our ancestors barely survived, then I don't see how we can be successful with odds and ends of their science."

He added, "I have an idea that the enemy ship is constructed of materials in which no pattern of destruction can be established."

The meaning of that shocked Jerrin. "Am I to understand that this first attack is being undertaken with the purpose of convincing me to support a *second* attack? And that it is this second attack you are building your hopes on?"

Clane hesitated, then nodded. "Yes," he said.

"What is the nature of your second plan?" Jerrin asked.

He grew pale as Clane outlined it. "You want us to risk the fleet merely as a support?"

Clane said simply, "What else is it good for?"

Jerrin was trembling, but he held his voice calm. "The role you have in mind for yourself to some extent shows how seriously you regard this matter. But, brother, you are asking me to risk the state. If you fail, they'll destroy cities."

Clane said, "The ship cannot be allowed to return home."

"Why not? It seems the simplest solution. They'll leave sooner or later."

Clane was tense. "Something happened," he said. "It was not a completely successful war for them thousands of years ago. They were driven off then, apparently not aware that they had caused irreparable damage to the solar system by destroying all its cities. If this ship gets back now, and reports that we are virtually helpless, they'll return in force."

"But why?" said Jerrin. "Why should they bother us?"

"Land."

The blood rushed to Jerrin's face, and he had a vision then of the fight that had taken place long ago. The desperate, deadly, merciless war of two races, utterly alien to each other, one seeking to seize, the other to hold, a planetary system. The picture was sufficient. He felt himself stiffening to the hard necessities. He straightened.

"Very well," he said in a ringing voice, "I wish to see this experiment. Proceed."

The metal case with the silvery ball rolling back and forth in it was brought to the center of the glade. It was the object Jerrin had watched them bring aboard at Clane's estate. He walked over to it, and stood looking down at it.

The ball rolled sedately first to one end, and then back again to the other. Its movement seemed without meaning. Jerrin put his hand down, glanced up to see if Clane objected to his action; and when Clane merely stood watching him, lowered his finger gingerly into the path of that glistening sphere.

He expected it to be shoved out of the way by a solid metal weight.

The ball rolled through it.

Into it, through it beyond it. There was no feeling at all, no sensation of substance. It was as if he had held his hand in empty air.

Repelled by its alienness, Jerrin drew back. "What is it?" he said with distaste.

The faintest of smiles came into Clane's face. "You're asking the wrong type of question," he said.

Jerrin was momentarily baffled, and then he remembered his military training. "What does it do?"

"It absorbs any energy directed at it. It converts all matter that it touches into energy, and then absorbs the energy."

"It didn't convert my finger into energy."

"It's safe to handle while it's in its case. It probably has a limitation on the amount of energy it will absorb, though I have yet to find what it is. That's what gives me hope that it just might be useful against the enemy."

"You're going to use it against *them?*"

Incredibly, it hadn't occurred to him that this was the weapon. He stared down at it, shocked; and the feeling—which had briefly gone away—that he was being made a fool of in some obscure fashion, returned. Jerrin looked around him unhappily. An armor-plated battleship a third of a mile

22

long floated in the mists to the southeast. Down here a dozen men stood in a forest glade. Nearby, lay the small, open-decked craft which had brought them from their own space-craft some ten miles away. The craft was unarmed except for a score of bowmen and spearmen.

Jerrin controlled himself. "When are you going to attack?"

"Now!"

Jerrin parted his lips to speak again, when he noticed that the silvery ball was gone from its case. With a start he looked up—and froze as he saw that it was floating in the air above Clane's head.

It was brighter now, and danced and blurred, and quivered like something alive. It was a shiningness, insubstantial yet palpable. Feather-light, it floated above the mutation's head, riding with his movements.

"Watch the ship!" Clane pointed.

The words and the movement were like a signal. The "ball" was abruptly gone from above his head. Jerrin saw it momentarily, high in the sky, a gleam against the dark bulk of the great ship. There was a flash of shiningness, and then the fantastic thing was back over Clane's head.

High above them, the great ship rode its invisible anchors, apparently unharmed.

Jerrin said with disappointment, "It didn't work?"

Clane waved at him, a spasmodic movement of his hand. "Wait!" he said. "There may be a counterattack."

The silence that followed did not last long.

A rim of fire appeared along a line of the ship running from the nose to the tail. Miles away in the forest, thunder rolled. It came near, and grew louder. A quarter of a mile away through the brush, there was a bright splash of fire, and then it was a quarter of a mile beyond them, on the other side.

Jerrin noticed that for just a moment while the thunder and flame threatened them, the ball was gone from above Clane. When he looked again, it was back in position, dancing, bobbing, blurring. Clane must have caught his distracted gaze, for he said, "They couldn't locate us so they plotted a curve, and struck at intervals along that line. The question is, will they notice that there was no explosion at one of the probable centers of the attack against them?"

Jerrin guessed then that the enemy had plotted an accurate

curve, and by some magic science had picked their exact position as one of the areas to attack.

And apparently the shining sphere had absorbed the energy of the attacking force.

He waited, tense.

After five minutes, there was still no sign of a further attack. At the end of twenty minutes, Clane said with satisfaction, "They seem to be satisfied with their counterattack. At least we know they're not superhuman. Let's go."

They boarded the small craft, slid along for a while slowly under a spread of tree branches, then turned through a narrow pass and so into a valley from which the big ship was not visible. As they picked up speed, Clane spoke again.

"I'd like to have a look at those captured craft that Raheinl sent you from Mars. The sooner we act the better. There may be retaliations."

Jerrin had been thinking about that, thinking of how deeply he was committed. An attack had been made, the enemy advised by active means that his presence was resented. The war was on, and there was no turning back.

He asked quietly, "When do you plan to make your second attack?"

IV

THE INVADING SHIP had fortunately not come nearer to the city of Linn than about a hundred and fifty miles. So it was natural that its first victim should not be the capitol. A large midland city received the first blow.

The bomb was dropped approximately twenty hours after Clane's attempt to destroy the alien with the sphere. It dropped on a city that had been evacuated except for street patrols and the looters who made the patrols necessary.

Dense clouds of smoke hid the damage and the disaster.

Less than half an hour later, a second city was struck by one of the colossal bombs, and the poisonous smoke rose up in its toadstool shape, infinitely deadly and irresistible.

The third city was struck an hour later, and the fourth shortly after noon. There was a pause then, and a host of small craft were seen to emerge from the giant. They explored the outer edges of the four gigantic smoke areas, and flew tantalizingly near Linnan patrol craft, as if trying to draw their fire.

When the news of this maneuver was brought to Clane, he sent a message to Jerrin.

Most Excellent Lord Leader:

It would appear that they were severely surprised by our attack yesterday, and are now trying to draw the fire of more such weapons as I turned against them, possibly with the hope of finding out exactly how much strength we can muster against them.

Having examined the machines captured from them by Raheinl, I am happy to report that one needs only minor repairs, and that we can launch our attack possibly tomorrow night.

Yours in hope,

Clane

Certain characteristics of the alien patrol craft puzzled Clane. As he supervised the work of the mechanics, he had to force himself by effort to concentrate on the coarser aspects of the task.

"If I have time," he told himself, "I'll investigate that attachment to the steering device."

The two machines lay side by side in one of his underground workshops. Each was approximately fifty feet long, and basically of very simple design. Their atomic motors were different from those in Linnan ships only in that they were more compact. The principle was the same. A block of treated metal exploded under control in rocket chambers.

For thousands of years machines thus powered had been flying through the atmosphere of the planets.

Jerrin arrived early in the afternoon of the day set for the attack. He was pale and earnest, and subdued. "Seventeen cities," he reported to Clane, "have now been destroyed. They are certainly inviting us to do everything we can."

Clane led him to the controls of the craft that had been repaired. "I've been experimenting," he said, "with a little attachment they have geared to the controls."

He bent down. "I have a map here," he said. "I want you to mark on it where the enemy ship now is, according to the latest reports."

Jerrin shrugged. "That's easy. It's lying to over—"

"*Don't tell me!*" Clane's words were quick and sharp, and had the desired effect. Jerrin gazed at him questioningly. Clane continued, "I have an idea in connection with this thing, so put your mark—and don't show it to me."

The older man accepted the map, and touched it with the point of a pencil as closely as possible to the exact location of the ship. He stepped back, and waited. Clane touched a button.

There was a faint throb as the motors sounded in the vast emptiness of the underground chamber. Under their feet, the craft turned slowly on its revolving platform, and steadied. The sound of the motors died away. Clane straightened.

"The nose is now pointing north by northeast. Draw a line on the map in that direction from this cavern."

Jerrin drew the line silently. It passed within a millimeter of the point where he had made his mark. "I don't understand," he said slowly. "You mean that this craft *knows* where the mother ship is?"

"It seems so, in a purely mechanical fashion of course."

"Then, very likely, the mother ship knows where it is."

Clane frowned. "It could be, but I doubt it. It would be quite complicated, and somewhat unnecessary, under normal circumstances, to keep track of hundreds of small craft. The small craft, however, must be able to return to the big machine."

He added, "If they knew where this craft was, I think they would have made some effort to get it back."

Jerrin shook his head. "The matter seems of minor importance. After all, we can locate the invader whenever we want to."

Clane said nothing to that. He had studied detailed reports of how these small ships entered into and emerged from their parent. And for hours now, a possibility had been growing on him.

It was not something that could be explained to a practical man. The whole concept of automatic machinery was as new as it was dazzling.

Zero hour was near.

It grew darker as they waited in the shelter of a mountain. Earlier, there had been desultory conversation between them, but now they were silent. From the men in the rear there came only an occasional mutter of sound.

The plan was made. The fleet had its orders. It was now only a matter of carrying out the attack itself.

"Halloo-oo!"

The call floated down from the rim of the peak. Jerrin straightened, and then, stepping close, embraced his brother. The darkness hid his tears. "Good luck," he said, "and forgive me for all the things that I have done or said or thought against you."

He stepped down into the darkness, where his own soldiers waited.

The mechanism of the captured Riss-craft functioned smoothly. Like a shadow, the machine rose, climbed, and flitted over the mountain top. Almost immediately, they were in the center of the battle.

The Linnan spaceships were attacking in groups of a hundred, and they came in waves. They were manned by skeleton crews, and they had two purposes: Engage if possible all the enemy's defenses by diving nose first into the torpedo-shaped invader. That was the first purpose.

It was believed the aliens would not care to have their interstellar ship rammed by hundreds of projectiles weighing thousands of tons each.

The second purpose of the attackers was for each crew to leave its ship in a small escape craft a few moments before contact. The theory was that the air would be so filled with lifeboats that the enemy would not notice their own captured machine approaching.

27

Clane's energy-absorbing sphere was expected to handle any direct attacks.

The sky flashed with flame. Everywhere, Linnan spaceships were burning and falling. Clane saw no lifeboats, however, and the first sick feeling that the men were not getting away, came. There was nothing to do, however, but go ahead.

The crash of Linnan spaceships striking the metal walls of the invader was almost continuous now; and there was no longer any doubt that the enemy's defenses were not capable of coping with such a complicated attack.

Clane thought tensely, "They'll have to leave. We won't have time to get near." It was a possibility that hadn't occurred to him, earlier.

He had taken it for granted that the big ship would be able to shrug off the Linnan attack without difficulty, and without moving from its position. Instead, it was being seriously hurt.

Beside him, his commanding officer whispered, "I think I see an opening."

Clane peered where the man was pointing, and saw it, too. He felt a chill, for it was directly ahead. Unmistakably, his craft was aiming toward it—or was being drawn toward it. It was possible that the automatic controls of his small machine had activated a door in the mother ship and that they would be able to enter without resistance. His own plan had been to force an entry with a tiny bomb, and it seemed to him he still preferred that method. The problem now was, was this a trap of those aboard, or was the process so automatic that no one paid any attention to newcomers?

It was a chance he had to take. The greatest danger was that the giant machine would start moving.

The light of the air lock proved deceptively dim. He was estimating that it was still more than a hundred feet away when there was a click. The machine slowed sharply, and he saw a blur of dully colored gray walls slide by on either side.

Doors flowed shut behind them and, in front, another set glided open. The small craft, with its thirty-five men aboard, moved sedately forward—and was inside the ship from the stars.

At his camp headquarters, where he had taken his family for refuge, Jerrin waited.

"They're still inside." That was the terse report from his chief field officer.

After nearly eighteen hours, the reality was a virtual death sentence. Jerrin blamed himself. "I should never have allowed him to go," he told Lilidel. "It's ridiculous that a member of our family should participate in direct assaults."

He had taken part in more than a hundred direct assaults himself, but he ignored that now. He also ignored the fact that only the man who controlled the energy sphere—Clane himself—could possibly carry out the attack that the latter had outlined to him.

Jerrin paced the floor of his headquarters study; and it was several minutes before he noticed that, for once, Lilidel had nothing to say. Jerrin stared at her narrowly, realizing grimly that she and those behind her were not displeased at what had happened.

"My dear," he said finally, "Clane's failure will have repercussions on the whole state. It will mark the beginning and not the end of our troubles."

Still she said nothing. And he saw that in this crisis she was not able to comprehend the issues. She had her own purposes, the purposes of a mother and of the agent of the group that worked through her. His mind went back to the choice the old Lady Lydia, his grandmother, had made in persuading her aging husband that *her* son should be the heir of Linn.

"I must make sure," Jerrin decided, "that the succession is never in Lilidel's giving. It's just about time, also, that I take more interest in the children. I can no longer trust what she has done with them."

That applied particularly to Calaj, his eldest son.

He looked again at his wife, and parted his lips to tell her that, if Clane was alive, he had the power to take over the government at will. He didn't say it. It would serve no useful purpose. In the first place she wouldn't believe it, and in the second it was not completely true. Government depended partly on the co-operation of the governed; and there were factors against Clane of which, fortunately—he was convinced—Clane himself was aware.

The meetings between them had made an amicable co-operation possible. Only an emergency, he was sure, would now alter the shape of things political in Linn.

I shall have to make a will, he thought. *If anything happened to me, if I should die—there must be no confusion.*

He felt oppressed. For a second time in less than a year, disaster had struck at the heart of the empire. First, Czinczar, the barbarian, and now the aliens. From the air he had seen the refugees streaming out of the concealing smoke of cities bombed before they were completely evacuated, and he was conscious of his inadequacy in the face of such a colossal catastrophe. It was that that decided him.

"I refuse," he said, "to believe that Clane has failed. If he has, then we are lost. And my awareness of that fact emphasizes once again his importance in a crisis. He is the only person qualified to handle a major emergency involving atomic energy. If he is still alive, I intend to do as follows."

She listened wide eyed as he explained about the will he planned to write. Abruptly, her face twisted with fury. "Why, you're mad," she breathed. "Are you serious? You're going to disinherit your own son?"

He gazed at her bleakly. "My dear," he said, "I want to make one thing clear to you and to your private army, for now and always. So long as I am the Lord Adviser, the state will not be regarded as a property which my children automatically inherit. It is too soon to decide whether Calaj has the qualities necessary for leadership. My impression of him is that he is an exceedingly emotional youth who gets his own way far too often. There is no sign as yet of that stability which I have, which Clane has, and which even Tews had to some degree."

The woman's face was softening. She came over to him. "I can see you're tired, darling. Please don't do anything rash until this crisis is past. I'll bring you a cup of tea—strong, the way you like it."

She brought the tea with trembling fingers, and went out with tears in her eyes. The liquid seemed unusually bitter even for his taste, but he sipped it as he began to dictate, first the will, then the letter to Clane. He recognized that he was taking a lot for granted, but his mood continued dark. And it was not until he had sealed the two articles, and put them among his public papers, that he realized that the strain of the past few days had affected his body. He felt very tired, even a little feverish.

He dismissed his secretary, and lay down on a cot under the window. Twenty minutes passed, and a door opened softly, so softly that the sleeper seemed undisturbed. Lilidel came in, took a cup in which the tea had been, and tiptoed out.

It was about an hour later when the intense silence of the room was again broken. The outer door was flung open. A staff officer burst across the threshold.

"Your excellency," he began breathlessly, "the invader has arrived above the camp."

The slim, uniformed body on the cot did not stir.

V

WHEN CLANE's "lift" boat came to rest inside the enemy ship, he saw after a moment that they were firmly held in a kind of metal incasement. The nose of the machine and half the body were buried in that enveloping cradle. All around him were other small craft similarly incased.

The craft had apparently slipped automatically into its own pigeonhole. And there was only one problem. Would the officer at the controls of the big machine notice that the lifeboat just in was one which had been captured on Mars by the human beings?

If he noticed, he gave no sign during the vital first minutes that followed.

There were high steps where the casement of the "pigeon-hole" ended. Up these steps Clane and his men climbed. They came to an empty corridor. Clane stopped short, hesitated, drew a deep breath—and sent the sphere on its death mission.

It flashed out of sight, came back, disappeared again, and

once more came back. For a third time, then, it glided off like a stroke of lightning.

This time it returned—sated.

They found no living creature of any kind. They wandered for hours before they were finally convinced that the huge ship had been captured during those few seconds by a simple process. The sphere had absorbed every alien being aboard. As soon as he was positive, Clane headed for the massive control room.

He was just in time to witness a strange mechanical phenomenon. A huge glassy plate, which had been lightless and soundless when he first passed through the control room, glittered with light flashes and stuttered with apparently meaningless sounds.

Clane took up a position behind a barrier, and, with the sphere bobbing above his head, watched alertly.

Abruptly, the lights on the plate steadied. A shape took form on it, and Clane was shaken as he recognized that the creature was of the same species as the monster that Czinczar had brought from Europa.

Only this one was alive in some curious picture fashion.

The creature stared from the plate into the control room, and it was nearly a minute before his gaze touched Clane. He said something in a series of low-pitched sounds that had no meaning for the mutant. Two other individuals came out of the vagueness behind him, and they also stared through the plate.

One of them gestured in unmistakable command, and roared something. There was a click, and the screen went blank. The sounds continued for a few seconds, and then they also faded.

Hesitantly, Clane ventured farther into the control room. He was trying to understand what he had seen. A picture of living aliens focused from some far place on a shining plate. It was a hard idea to grasp, but he had the sinking conviction that other living aliens now knew what had happened to the first of their ships to reach Earth.

In one mental jump he had to try to comprehend the possibility that communication could be established by other means than smoke signals, light flashes from strategically located mirrors, and courier ships. What he had seen indicated that such communication was possible not only over the face of a planet, but across the gulf of space between stars.

It changed everything. It changed the whole situation. Capture of this one ship actually meant nothing. Other aliens knew that the defense forces of the solar system had failed to protect their cities. They would be puzzled by the seizure of their ship, but it was doubtful if they would be seriously alarmed.

What one ship had almost accomplished, a fleet would surely be able to do—effortlessly. That would be their attitude; and Clane, swiftly estimating the defense possibilities of the solar system, did not doubt the ability of a powerful force of enemy ships to do anything they pleased.

The entire distance-vision incident was enormously significant. Gloomily, he began to study the control system of the big machine. Nearly four hours went by before he was satisfied that he could guide it for atmospheric travel.

Certain functions of the intricate control board baffled him completely. It would take time and study to master this ship.

He headed the ship for Jerrin's headquarters.

He landed in a lifeboat that trailed the fluttering victory flags of Linn, and in a few minutes was admitted to where Jerrin lay dead.

That was about an hour after the body was discovered.

As he gazed down at his dead brother, Lord Clane noticed almost immediately the evidence of poisoning. Shocked, he stepped back from the cot, and looked down at the scene, trying to assess it as a whole.

The widow Lilidel was on her knees with one arm flung in an apparent agony of grief over the corpse. She seemed anxious rather than grieved, and there was just a hint of calculation in the way her eyes were narrowed. She was tearless.

The tableau interested Clane. He had had innumerable reports about the group that had used this woman to influence Jerrin, and there was a time when he had even intended to warn Jerrin against her.

He found himself wondering where her eldest son, the incredible Calaj, was.

It required only a moment for that wonder to focus into a sharp picture of the potentialities of this situation. He had a sudden vision of Calaj already on his way to Golomb, the little town outside Linn to which the Patronate as well as other government departments had been transferred. Given advance warning, the group behind Lilidel—many well-known Patrons among them—might seize the occasion to proclaim the boy Lord Adviser.

There was explosive material here for a bloody struggle for power. Unless the right action were taken, rumors would spread that Jerrin had been murdered. Some of the rumors would point to the widow, others at Clane himself. Supporters of his own who had reluctantly accepted the noble Jerrin would very possibly refuse to agree that a youth of seventeen should be put into power by their worst enemies. Civil war was not improbable.

Jerrin's secretary, General Marak—a secret Clane supporter—touched Clane's arm, and whispered in his ear. "Your excellency, here are copies of very important documents. I would not swear that the originals are still available."

A minute later Clane was reading his brother's last will. Then he read the personal letter, of which the essential sentence was, "I trust my dear wife and children to your care."

Clane turned and gazed at the widow. Her eyes met his briefly, flashed with hatred; and then she lowered them, and thereafter gave no sign that she was aware of his presence.

He guessed that his appearance on the scene was unexpected.

It was time for decision. And yet, he hesitated. He glanced at the high staff officers in the room, all Jerrin men, and still he could not make up his mind. He had a picture in his brain larger than anything that was happening in this room—or on this planet. A picture of a mighty alien fleet heading from some far star system to avenge the capture of their exploring ship. Of course that would be only an additional incitement. Their real purpose would be to destroy every human being in the solar system, and seize all of man's planets—while men fought each other for the petty stakes of governmental power.

With fingers that trembled slightly, Clane folded the two

documents and put them in his pocket. Standing here in the presence of his dead brother, so recently become a friend, he hated the political knowledge that made him think automatically, *I'll have to try to get the originals, in case I ever want to use them.*

The revulsion grew stronger. With narrowing eyes and grim face, he gazed not only at this scene before him, but at the world of Linn outside—the intricate association of direct vision and sharp, perceptive memory, the scene he was seeing and all the scenes he had ever witnessed. He remembered his own schemes over the years, his emotional joy in political maneuvering; and now in one burst of insight, recognized it all for the childish nonsense it had been.

His lips moved. Under his breath he murmured, "Beloved brother, I am shamed, for I knew enough to know better."

It seemed to him, then, that Jerrin had been a greater man than he. All his life, Jerrin had treated politics and politicians with disdain, devoting himself to the hard realities of a military man in an age when war was inescapable.

"Can I do less?" The question quivered in his mind like a flung knife vibrating in the flesh.

Then he saw that he was being sentimental in making comparisons. For his problem was on a level that Jerrin could hardly even have imagined. There was power here for him if he wanted it. All the schemes of Lilidel and her group could not stop him from seizing control by sheer force. Without shame, without modesty, he recognized that he was *the* man of science in Linn.

Clearly, sharply, he perceived his pre-eminence, the enormous stability of his mind, the acuteness of his understanding. Somehow he had it, and others hadn't. It made it necessary now for him to reject the highest office in the land— because he had a duty to the whole race of man. A duty that grew out of his knowledge of the titanic danger.

He could expect no one else to evaluate the extent of that danger, least of all this venal, childish woman and those behind her.

Abruptly, angrily decisive, Clane turned and beckoned General Marak. The latter came forward quickly. To him, Clane whispered, "I would advise you to leave this room with me. I could not otherwise answer for the life of a man

35

who knows what is in these documents." He tapped his pocket, where the copy of Jerrin's will reposed.

It was unfortunate, but that was the grim reality. Intrigue and sudden death.

Without a word to any of the others present, he turned and left the room, Marak following close behind. His problem would be to restrain his more ardent followers from trying to seize power in his name.

And save a world that was almost mindless with corruption.

A few hours later, he landed at his estate. His guards' captain met him.

"Your excellency," he said curtly, "the sphere and its container have been stolen."

"The sphere gone!" said Clane. His spirit sagged like a lead weight.

In a few minutes, he had the story. The guards of the sphere had apparently been ambushed by a larger force.

The captain finished, "When they didn't get back here on schedule, I investigated personally. I found their bodies at the bottom of a canyon. All of them were dead.

Clane's mind was already beyond the crime, seeking the culprit. And swiftly, he focused on one man.

"Czinczar," he said aloud, savagely.

VI

FOR CZINCZAR and his men, defeat at the hands of Lord Clane a few months previously had not been a complete disaster. Before actually ordering his army to surrender, that remarkable logician examined his situation.

At the worst, he himself would not be killed immediately but would be saved for public execution. His men, of course, would be sold into slavery—unless he could persuade Lord

Clane to let the army remain a unit. To do that, he must convince the mutation that such a force might be useful to him.

Since his reasoning was soundly based, everything happened as he had hoped it would. Clane transferred the barbarian army, together with a number of crack rebel slave units, to an easily defendable mountain territory. Having regained control of the invincible sphere of energy, the mutation considered himself in control of the situation. He even suspected correctly that Czinczar had held a number of spaceships out in space, where they could still be contacted.

At the time he informed the barbarian leader, "These ships could provide you with transportation to return to your planet. But I warn you, make no such move without my permission. You must know that I can seek you out and destroy you at any time."

Czinczar had no doubt of it. And besides, he had no desire to return to Europa. Great events were in the making, and he intended to be in the center of them.

He began his preparations boldly.

Single spaceships were fitted out for forays. The men assigned to them shouted their disapproval when informed they must shave off their beards, but the leader was adamant. Singly and in the dark of night, spaceships landed at carefully selected points as far as possible from the city of Linn. Out of them sprang bare-faced men dressed like ordinary Linnans. They killed men only, slaves as well as Linnans—and helped themselves over a period of many months to vast supplies of grain, fruit, vegetables, meat, and all the metal and wood that an army might need.

The prisoners had been assigned a minimum existence diet by Clane. Within a week of the surrender they were eating off the fat of the land. From every fire on the mountains came the odor of roasting meat. Within a few weeks there were several women to attend to each fire. Czinczar issued orders that only slave women should be brought to the camp, and that any Linnan women captured by mistake should be killed.

Everyone agreed that this was wise, but suspiciously no women were executed. It seemed clear to Czinczar that the Linnan women, when informed of the alternatives, were only too anxious to masquerade as slaves. And so the purpose of the bloodthirsty threat was served. A huge camp, that might have been disorderly in the extreme, operated for months on a high level of efficiency.

And, because of the tremendous dislocation of normal Linnan life, first as a result of the barbarian invasion and then because of the alien invader, their violent actions went almost unnoticed; their existence was almost literally unsuspected.

The arrival of the invader made possible even bolder activity. In broad daylight barbarian ships would land at the outskirts of cities, and in small groups penetrate past the guardposts without being challenged. These small spying units brought back information from widely scattered points to one of the keenest military minds of the age. As a result, Czinczar knew before the event that an attack was going to be made against the invading ship. And he also knew the nature of it.

On the night of the attack he was fully aware of the tremendous issues at stake. He personally accompanied the men who crouched within bow and arrow range of the coffin-like structure which acted as a container for the sphere of energy. He waited until the sphere vanished into the darkness toward the gigantic enemy ship. Then he gave his command. The little group of barbarians swept down upon the half hundred guards around the container.

The darkness echoed with the horrified cries of men bloodily surprised by a superior force. But silence followed swiftly. The barbarians disposed of the dead guards by rolling them over a nearby cliff. Then they settled themselves tensely to wait for the sphere.

It came suddenly. One instant there was nothing; the next, the silver ball was rolling sedately to and fro. Czinczar gazed down at it, startled. It was not the first time he had seen it, but now he realized some of its powers.

Aloud, he said, "Bring the telescope. I might as well have a look inside this thing while we're waiting."

That was a new idea; and the method used was very rough. Two men poked the long, narrow telescope into the outer "skin" of the sphere, and then walked along at a steady pace beside it. It was a problem in timing, and Czinczar's part was the most difficult. He walked beside the telescope, one eye glued to the eyepiece; and the trick was to establish a rhythm of backward and forward movement.

His first view was so different from anything he might have expected that his vision blurred, and he fell out of step. He organized himself, and looked again. Oddly, the surprise was almost as great, as if his mind had already rejected what it first saw.

He saw a starry universe. He stepped back in confusion, striving to grasp the awful magnitude, the fantastic reality. Then once more he fell in step, and gazed. By the time he straightened up again, he was trying to interpret what he had seen.

The sphere, he decided, was a "hole" in space. Baffled, he stared down at it, as it rolled back and forth. How could a silvery ball-like object be an opening into anything?

He motioned the men to take the telescope away, and then punched his finger into the sphere. He felt nothing at all, no resistance, no sensation.

The finger swelled a little finally, and he remembered that meteor miners had proved space was not cold, but that it was vital to wear an air-tight pressure suit. Lack of pressure would have caused his finger to bloat.

He wondered if he had reached into some depth of space. A finger poking out of nowhere into a vacuum. Thoughtfully, he walked away from the sphere and sat down on a rock. In the east, the sky was beginning to lighten, but still he sat there, still his men waited in vain for the order to leave. He intended to give Clane every opportunity of using the sphere against the aliens.

As the sun edged over the jagged horizon, he stood up briskly, and had the container and the sphere transported to a waiting ship. The vessel had instructions to climb right out of the atmosphere, and take up an orbit around Earth.

Czinczar remembered sharply how Clane had had to come to the city Linn to make use of the sphere against himself. And there was the fact that each time it was used, it had to be transported near the object against which it was to be employed.

Accordingly, the greatest weapon ever conceived was in his possession.

He was not satisfied. Restlessly, he paced the room which

was his headquarters, and over and over again examined the facts of his position. Years ago, he had discovered the basic secret of power and success. And now, because the pattern was not complete, he was uneasy.

Men came and went from his room. Spies bringing information. The invading ship was captured. Jerrin was dead. Clane had refused to take advantage of the death, and had instructed his supporters not to oppose the plan to make Calaj the Lord Adviser.

When then the man who brought that latest bit of news had gone, Czinczar shook his head in wonder, and for the first time in all these months something of his terrible tension let up. He himself wouldn't have had the courage *not* to seize power at such an opportune moment. Nor could he visualize the logic of it—even so, the actuality seemed superhuman.

It made him indecisive. He had intended to make an effort to seize the gigantic invader ship when Clane was not on it. With clocklike precision his men completed the preliminaries —but he did not give the final order.

On the sixth day after the death of Jerrin, a messenger came from Clane commanding him aboard the captured giant. Czinczar suspected the worst, but he had no alternative short of open resistance. Since that would quickly bring the main Linnan armies against him, he decided to trust himself to Clane and to his own analysis of the situation.

At the appointed hour, accordingly, Czinczar and his staff flew in a strongly escorted patrol vessel to Clane's estate. The alien ship floated high above, as they stepped to the ground.

A few guards lounged around. Nowhere was there sign of a force large enough to defend the battleship from a determined air attack. Looking up, Czinczar saw that several dozen air locks were open in the ship, and that a thin but steady traffic moved to and from the openings. It was a picture that his spies had reported in considerable detail, and it baffled Czinczar now as it had earlier. The ship looked helpless, wide open to assault. The very extent of that helplessness had made him hesitate. It was still hard to credit that Clane could be so negligent, but now the barbarian leader silently cursed himself for his failure to take advantage of a military possibility.

For the first time in his grim career he had missed an opportunity. He had a premonition of disaster.

He watched with narrowed eyes, as one of Clane's officers came up. The man saluted the barbarian commanders with stiff formality, and then bowed to Czinczar.

"Your excellency, will you and your staff please follow me?"

Czinczar expected to be led toward the estate residence, which was visible over a low hill about a third of a mile to the south. Instead, the Linnan officer guided them to a small stone building, half hidden among thick undergrowth. Once more he saluted and bowed.

"If you will step inside one by one," he said, "so that the machine can take a"—he hesitated over the word—"photograph of you." He added hurriedly, "Lord Clane asked me to assure you that this is essential; otherwise it would be impossible for you to approach the *Solar Star.*"

Czinczar said nothing, nor did he immediately allow himself to examine the meaning of the words. He motioned his officers to go in ahead of him, and watched curiously as each man in turn entered, disappeared for a moment, and then came into sight and through the door. Since he did not ask them, they all knew better than to volunteer information.

Presently, it was his turn. Unhurriedly, Czinczar stepped through the door. He found himself in a room that was bare except for a chair and a table, and the instrument that rested on the table. The chair was occupied by an officer, who rose to his feet and bowed, as Czinczar entered.

The barbarian acknowledged the greeting, then stared curiously at the instrument. It looked as if it had been torn from its metal casing. The metal was fused where it had been cut with torches. Czinczar noted the point in passing, saw also that the machine itself seemed to consist principally of a telescopelike protuberance complete with lens. He turned to the attendant.

"What does it do?" he asked.

The officer was polite. "According to Lord Clane, sir, it takes photographs."

"But that's only another word for portrait," said Czinczar. "Do you mean the machine has made a portrait of me? If so, where is it?"

The attendant's cheeks were slightly flushed. "Your ex-

41

cellency," he confessed, "I know nothing more. Lord Clane asked me to refer all interrogators to him personally." He added, somewhat pointedly, "I believe that he will expect you, now that you are through here."

Czinczar was persistent. "I didn't see you do anything."

"It's automatic, sir. Anyone who stands in front of it is photographed."

"If such a photograph," said the barbarian, "is necessary before I can approach the ship, how was it that Lord Clane and his men were able to enter the vessel a week ago, and capture it, without having their photographs taken?"

It was a rhetorical question, and he scarcely heard the other's protestation of ignorance. Silently, he left the little building, and followed the first officer to a larger liftboat, which was in the act of settling to the ground half a hundred feet distant.

In a few minutes they were whisked up to one of the openings. The liftboat glided through, and gently nosed into a slot. Czinczar stepped out with the others, hesitated as he saw the double lines of guards drawn up to receive them, and then, with the chill of the welcome already upon him, walked wordlessly along a corridor toward a huge door. As he crossed the threshold, and saw the tremendous gallows that had been erected against the far wall, he stopped involuntarily.

The pause was momentary. Imperturbably, he walked forward, straight to the foot of the gallows. He sat down on a lower step, pulled out a notebook, and began to write a farewell address. He was still writing it when, out of the corner of his eyes, he saw Clane come in. He stood up, and bowed.

The slim young man came over to him, and without any preliminaries said, "Czinczar, you have a simple choice. Produce the sphere, or hang."

"Sphere?" said the barbarian finally. He hoped he sounded properly surprised, but he did not doubt the seriousness of his situation. There were rough minutes ahead.

Clane made an impatient gesture, hesitated, and then grew visibly calmer. "Czinczar," he said slowly, "your skillful reorganization of your forces the last few months had just about decided me to use you in a major enterprise."

The barbarian bowed once more, but his eyes narrowed at the revelation that his activities were known to the mutation. Czinczar neither underestimated nor overestimated the fact. He recognized both the weakness and strength of Lord Clane's position. The great weakness was that he depended too much on himself. He was at the mercy of people who had little or no idea of the relative importance of his possessions or his actions.

And so, during the barbarian assault on Linn, the attackers had seized Clane's house with all its valuable scientific equipment, including the sphere of force. Not knowing the tremendous potentialities of the sphere, they had made the mistake of trying to use it and the other equipment as bait to trap Clane. And thus had let him get near it—and trapped themselves.

The secrecy that made such things possible was a form of strength. But obviously, once the pattern was understood, the solution was simple. Watch Clane's movements. He could not be everywhere at once. Like other human beings, he needed sleep; he had to take time off for eating. It was impossible for him to be alert continuously.

The fact that he had allowed the barbarian force to reorganize was no evidence that he was capable of foreseeing all the possible eventualities of such an act. His successful capture of the sphere was evidence of that.

Once more, it was Clane who broke the silence. "As you know," he said, "I have defended you from the fate that is normally dealt out to individuals who have the audacity to invade Linn. The policy of executing such leaders may or may not be a deterrent on other adventurers; possibly it is. I saved you from it, and one of your first acts is to betray me by stealing a weapon which you have not the knowledge to use yourself."

It seemed to Czinczar that it was time to make a denial. "I don't know what you're talking about," he protested in his most open-faced fashion. "Has the sphere been stolen?"

Clane seemed not to hear. He went on grimly, "I cannot say honestly that I have ever admired you. You have discovered a simple technique of power, and you keep following the pattern. I personally am opposed to so much killing, and

43

I really believe it is possible to reach the heights of power in *any* state, however governed, without stabbing a single person in the back."

He paused; he took a step backward. His eyes were merciless as they stared straight into Czinczar's. He said curtly, "Enough of this talk. Do you yield up the sphere, or do you hang?"

Czinczar shrugged. The pressure of the deadly threat tensed every muscle in his body. But in his tremendously logical way he had analyzed the potentialities of his theft of the sphere and he still stood by that analysis.

"I know nothing of this," he said quietly. "I have not got the sphere. I did not even know it was stolen until this minute. What is this enterprise on which you planned to use me? I'm sure we can come to an agreement."

"There are no agreements," said Clane coldly, "until I get the sphere." He went on, "However, I see that you are convinced that I won't hang the man who has it, so let us proceed to the actuality. Will you climb the gibbet yourself or do you need assistance?"

Since there could be no effective opposition, Czinczar turned around, climbed the steps to the top of the gallows and without waiting for the hangman to help him, slipped the rope over his head. He was pale now, in spite of his confidence. For the first time it struck him that the dazzling career of Czinczar, the onetime scribe who had made himself absolute ruler of the barbarians of Europa, was about to end.

He saw that Clane had motioned the executioner, a Linnan noncommissioned officer, to come forward. The man took up his position beside the lever that would open the trapdoor, and turned to watch Clane, who had raised his arm. The mutation stood tautly in that striking position, and said, "A last chance, Czinczar. The sphere or death."

"I haven't got it," said Czinczar in a steady voice, but with finality.

Inexorably, Clane's arm swept down. Czinczar felt the trap under him collapse. And then—

He was falling.

VII

He dropped about a foot, and landed so jarringly that his body vibrated with pain. The tears started to his eyes. He blinked them away. When his vision cleared, he saw that he was standing on a second trapdoor, which had been built below the first.

He grew aware of scuffling somewhere near. He glanced around. His staff officers were struggling with the Linnan guards, trying to reach him. Czinczar hesitated, wondering if perhaps he and they should not attempt to make a fight to the death.

He shook his head, ever so slightly. The fact that he was still alive underlined his own hard convictions. He raised his golden voice, and presently the barbarian officers ceased their struggles, and stood sullenly looking up at him.

Czinczar spoke directly at them, indirectly at Clane. "If my life is really in danger," he said with resonant positivity, "it will be because Lord Clane has lost his good sense. That would apply even if I had the sphere—"

He realized that Clane would regard the words as an admission, and he glanced coolly at the mutation, inviting comment. Clane scowled; but he picked up the challenge after a moment.

"Suppose that you did have the sphere," he said mildly, "why does that protect you?"

"Because," said Czinczar, and his golden voice had never been steadier, "if I have it, so long as I am alive, you would still have a chance of getting it back. If I die, then that chance goes forever."

"If you had it," said Clane in a grim but ironic voice, "why would you want to hold on to it, knowing that you cannot make any use of it?"

45

"I would first have to make an investigation," was the barbarian's reply. "After all, you learned how to use it without having any previous knowledge of its operation."

"I had a book," Clane flashed, "and besides I have some knowledge of the nature and structure of matter and energy."

"Perhaps," said Czinczar coolly, "I could get hold of the book—such things do happen."

"I memorized this particular book," said Clane, "and then destroyed it."

Czinczar was politely incredulous. "Perhaps, my agents could discover the place where you burned it," he said. "Or, if I sent them into the homes of the gods, they might find another book."

He realized that tension was building up again, and that no verbal byplay would settle this argument. Clane was stiffening, his eyes narrowing. "Czinczar," he said sharply, "*if* you had this sphere, and you knew that you couldn't ever find out how to use it, would you still hold on to it, knowing the danger that is building up for the human race?"

The barbarian drew a deep breath. He expected a violent reaction. "Yes," he said.

"Why?" Clane was visibly holding himself under control.

"Because," said Czinczar, "I have no confidence in a man who refuses repeatedly to accept power, and who thus rejects the only means by which he can control and direct the defense against a possible invader. And, besides, the sphere is obviously worthless against the Riss."

Clane seemed not to hear that last. "Suppose I told you that I refused to take power because I have a plan of much greater scope."

"I recognize power," said Czinczar flatly, "not the grandiose schemes of a man who is now virtually impotent."

"My plan," said Clane, "is of such scope that I dare not tell it to a man of your rigid attitudes, for fear that you would regard it as impractical. For once I don't think your imagination could appreciate the possibilities."

"Try me."

"When I have the sphere," said Clane, "and not one second before. As for my being impotent, please note that I have the ship."

Czinczar was scornful. "What are you going to do with it—attack the legal government and make the people love you? That isn't the way a mutation can operate. For you and for your group the moment for taking over the government is past. It will probably not come again until the Riss attack, and by then anything you can do may be too late."

He went on, in an even more violent tone, "Lord Clane, you have been a grave disappointment to me. Your failure has placed my troops and myself in grave danger, because very soon now the *legal* government of Linn will demand that you turn us over, and of course you will also be required to turn over the ship. If you refuse, then for the first time in your life you will be out in the open as a rebel. From that moment on, your days are numbered."

Clane was smiling humorlessly. "I can see," he said, "that you are at your old game of political intrigue, and I am utterly impatient with such childish nonsense. The human race is in deadly danger, and I refuse to argue with anyone who plots and schemes for advantage under such circumstances. Men must mature or die."

He turned aside, and said something to one of the officers who stood near him. The man nodded, and once more Clane faced Czinczar.

The barbarian braced himself for the next step of torture.

Clane said curtly, "Please remove the noose from around your neck, and come over to the tank in the corner to your left."

As he slipped the rope over his head, Czinczar studied the tank. It was a large concrete affair, and he had noticed it when he first came in. It looked enigmatic; he couldn't imagine its purpose.

He was thinking furiously as he came down from the gallows. He said to Clane, "I'm really very persuadable. Why not tell me your plan? I can't give you the sphere as evidence of my good faith because I haven't got it."

Clane merely shook his head impatiently. Czinczar accepted the rejection, and said matter-of-factly, "Do I climb into the tank?"

Clane said, "Take a look inside, and you'll see the arrangement."

Czinczar climbed up curiously, and looked down. The tank

47

was quite deep and it was empty. At the bottom was a simple hand pump, and there were two chains with clamps fastened to rings imbedded in the concrete floor.

He lowered himself gingerly into the tank, and waited for instructions. He looked up and saw that Clane was looking down at him over the edge.

"Fasten the chain clamps around your ankles," instructed the mutation.

Czinczar did so. They clicked shut with a metallic finality. The metal felt heavy against his flesh and even uncomfortable.

"The chains," explained the mutation, "will hold you down to the bottom of the tank, so that when the water comes in you'll have to pump it out if you want to prevent yourself from drowning." He added, "You can see the approach is very simple. The pump operates easily. The choice you make will be entirely your own. You live or die by your own effort, and at any time you can stop the entire process by agreeing to turn over the sphere. There comes the water now."

It swirled around Czinczar's legs, bubbling up noisily. It was lukewarm, so it felt rather pleasant. Czinczar sat down on the floor, and glanced up at Clane.

"May I make a request?" he asked.

"Does it include handing over the sphere?"

"No."

"Then I'm not interested."

"It's the pump," said Czinczar. "Its presence makes me unhappy. Will you please have it taken out?"

Clane shook his head. "A few minutes from now you might be very happy to have it there." Nevertheless, there was an anxious look in his eyes as he spoke. The reaction was clearly one that he had not expected.

He finished, "If you change your mind at any time, you'll find that the pump can quickly reduce the level of the water."

Czinczar did not answer. The water was swirling around his neck. In a minute it closed over his mouth. He found himself involuntarily relaxing so that he could float up a little. He tensed with the expectation of the physical horror that was now only minutes away.

Presently, he was standing up, and he could feel the weight of the chain on his ankles. There was no doubt but that he had reached the limit of that particular method of escaping. And still the water surged higher.

It came up to his mouth again, then his nose. He held his breath as it rose up over his eyes and covered his head. And then, abruptly, he couldn't hold it any longer. Explosively he exhaled—and inhaled.

There was a knifelike pain in his chest, but that was all. The water tasted flat and unpleasant, not as if he was drinking it. Finally, there was no sensation at all. Darkness closed over his consciousness.

When he came to, he was lying over a barrel. He had never felt more miserable in his life. And they were still squeezing water out of him.

He was coughing. Every explosive discharge wracked his body. The pain of returning life was immeasurably greater than the pain of death. But even he realized presently that he would live.

They carried him to a cot, and there after an hour or so, he began to feel normal again. Clane came in alone, pulled up a chair, and sat silently regarding him.

"Czinczar," he said at last, "I am reluctantly compelled to admire your bravery. I despise the animal-like astuteness behind it."

Czinczar waited. He refused to believe that his travail was over.

"You have proved once more," said the mutation bitterly, "that a courageous man who is prepared to take calculated risks on the low level of political intrigue can conquer even death. I hate the stupid logic which makes you feel that you have to keep the sphere. If you persist in that madness, we are all dead men."

"If I had this sphere," said Czinczar, "then the logical thing for you to do in a moment of crisis would be for you to forget self and tell me how to work it."

Czinczar spoke in a precise tone, conscious of how dangerous the statement was. It was his first admission by implication of his own vast ambitions. For it was obvious that if he ever learned how to use the sphere, he would thereafter be in a position to seize power at will, and take control of any state.

It also implied that, according to his analysis of Clane's

character, the other might actually allow him to have control of the sphere in an emergency involving the destiny of the human race as distinct from any nation.

Clane was shaking his head. "It won't happen, my friend. I do not expect that the sphere will ever again by itself be useful against the Riss. I won't tell you why."

Czinczar was silent. He had hoped, not too optimistically, that somewhere along the line he would receive a clue about the operation of the sphere. But the information he was getting made the problem seem more, not less, difficult.

Clane continued, "It might appear that I was very careless with the sphere. But long ago I discovered that I could not be everywhere at once. And of course, I repeat, it's quite useless to anyone else. It works on the basis of a mathematical formula relating to the release of atomic energy, and I question whether anyone in the solar system other than myself even knows that there is such a formula."

Czinczar had his clue, and it was bitter to take. He said at last, "What are your plans for me, as of this moment?"

Clane hesitated. When he finally spoke, there was an edge of fire in his tone. "For the past few months," he said, "I have tolerated your murderous forays because I question whether we could have got together such a vast total of food and other supplies by any legal method in my control."

He paused, then continued, "I question also whether it would have been possible to get so many women together without using methods similar to yours. For my purposes, the women are as important as the food."

Once more he paused. And Czinczar had time to feel chagrined. He had thought he knew something of the intricate workings of this man's mind. But now, briefly, he was beyond his depth, and he had the empty conviction that he had been outplayed at his own devious game.

It was a startling thought that his secret forays would now be used for the benefit of Clane's plan. The mutation continued.

"Here is what I want you to do. Tomorrow, the *Solar Star* will fly over to your camp. You will begin to load your equipment aboard the lower decks—there are twenty of them, each capable of holding about ten thousand people and their supplies; so there'll be plenty of room for your entire army and the women."

Czinczar said, "Once I have such a force aboard, what's to prevent me from taking over the ship?"

Clane smiled grimly. "The twenty upper decks are already occupied by a well armed Linnan army group, all young married men accompanied by their wives. Except on the officer level, there will be no liaison between the two groups. In fact, except for an entrance from your headquarters all connecting doors will be sealed."

Czinczar nodded, half to himself. It sounded effective. Every defense of that kind could of course be overcome by bold and astute planning. But that scarcely concerned him now. There was an implication here of a tremendous journey about to be undertaken, and that dominated his thought.

"Where are we going?" he asked sharply. "To one of the outer moons?"

"Wait and see," said Clane coolly.

He stood up, with a frown. "Enough of this. You have your instructions. I have to make a vital journey to the capitol. I want you and your forces to be aboard and ready for flight one week from today. And if you can for once rise above the moronic military idiocy that guides your reasoning, bring the sphere along." His tone was one of suppressed anger.

Czinczar stared at him thoughtfully. "My friend," he said, "you're being emotional. There *is* no escape from political intrigue. This that you suddenly despise is the human environment. The environment of human passion, human ambition. There never has been, and never will be any other climate for you to operate in. A man succeeds or fails to the extent that he can understand and control the unrelenting drives of others of his kind. If he tries to abandon intrigue, the tide will wash over him and his plans as if they never existed. Beware."

He finished automatically, "I haven't got the sphere."

VIII

THE ARROW came out of the darkness, whizzed past Clane's head, and lodged in the shoulder of a guardsman.

The man screamed throatily, and clutched at the thin, vibrating wand. A companion leaped to his aid. Other soldiers dived into the alleyway. There was the sound of squealing, almost feminine in its high-pitched alarm and annoyance. Presently, a group of soldiers stalked out of the darkness, dragging a slim, resisting, boyish form.

The injured man, meanwhile, succeeded in tearing the arrow from his flesh. More frightened than damaged, he stood there cursing in a deep, bass voice.

Men were hurrying back from farther along the street. Torches flamed and guttered in the night wind. In that smoky, malodorous atmosphere, the changing patterns of dim light gave only flashing glimpses of faces and bodies. Clane stood silent, displeased with the milling excitement. Presently, when the turmoil showed no sign of abating, he called to an officer, and in a minute a path was cleared for him. Along it the guards dragged the prisoner.

Somebody shouted, "It's a woman!"

The discovery echoed back among the men. Curses of amazement sounded. The woman, or boy—it was hard to decide which in that dim light—ceased struggling. And then settled the question of gender by speaking.

"Let me go, you filthy rats! I'll have you whipped for this. I wish to speak to Lord Clane."

The voice, despite its vicious tone, was feminine. What was more surprising, the accent was that cultivated at the schools where young ladies of noble birth were taught.

The recognition startled Clane out of the icy calm into which the attempt on his life had thrown him. He took a for granted that the attempt *had* been on him, and not on the guard who had actually been struck. He assumed automatically that the assassin was an agent of the group behind Lilidel.

The names of her immediate superiors would have to be wheedled out of her, now that the assassination had failed. That was a natural development, and it concerned him only incidentally. What disturbed him was that she had evidently not considered the serious consequences of her act. In accepting the assignment, she couldn't have known a long established method of dealing with woman assassins. They were turned over to the soldiers.

He stared at her with troubled eyes. It was probably an illusion of the unsteady light, but she seemed little more than a child. At a maximum, he put her age at eighteen. Her eyes gleamed with the passionate fire of a willful youngster. Her mouth was full and sensuous.

He shrugged as he realized that he was yielding her up in his own mind to the punishment established by long practice. He who had recently set himself against so many old customs, could not now afford to offend his own private guard. Slowly, he stiffened to the inevitabilities of the situation.

Because he was angry at her for the decision she was forcing on him, he said with grim curtness, "Who are you?"

"I won't talk here," she said.

"What's your name?"

She hesitated; then, apparently recognizing the hostility in his voice, she said sullenly, "Madelina Corgay."

The identification gave him his second major pause. For it was an old and famous name in Linn. Generals and Patrons had borne that name into the field of battle and with it had signed the laws of the country. The father of this girl, Clane recalled, had died fighting on Mars, a year before. As a war hero, his daughter's action would be excused.

Clane was chagrined to realize that he was already thinking of the political repercussions. But it would be folly to blind himself to the fact that this incident could be highly dangerous to him. He shook his head angrily. With Calaj already voted Lord Adviser, and scheduled to make his triumphal entry into this capitol city of Linn tomorrow morning, the young man's supporters might well make an issue of an affair like this. And yet he had to take into account the expectations of the guards, who would not be interested in excuses. Fortunately, an intermediate decision was possible.

"Bring her along," he said. "I shall question her when we reach our destination."

No one demurred. It was expected that there would be a period of questioning. The crisis would come later.

Clane gave the necessary orders. Presently the procession was moving again along the street.

Several weeks had gone by since the capture of the invading ship, and it was more than six months since the defeat of Czinczar and his barbarian army from Europa, that distant and little known moon of Jupiter. The Linnan world was still in the process of settling down from those two near catastrophes. But already the survivors were forgetting how great the danger had been. From all parts of the empire the ever-louder voices of discontent echoed.

Commercial interests protested that Czinczar never had been a real threat. And that in any event the danger had been a product of gross negligence by the government. Jerrin had overruled previous objections, but now that Jerrin was dead there was a determined movement under way to nullify the decree which Clane had proclaimed during the barbarian invasion, freeing all loyal slaves. The feverish fury of numberless individuals dispossessed of valuable servants mounted with each passing day. And several ugly rumors had come to Clane that there would probably have been no disasters in the first place if a mutation had not been tolerated for so long in the family of the lord leaders.

That was a direct attack at himself, and one which he could not fight by any means known to him. This was particularly true since he had prevented his supporters from opposing the Patronate vote that gave the Lord Advisership to young Calaj.

Alarmed by the direction the public rage was taking, several of Clane's adherents had already regretted that they had allowed him to persuade them. It was now necessary, they claimed, for him to act before the Lord Adviser Calaj actually arrived in the capitol.

It was just such a scheme that had brought Clane on this night journey through the streets of sleeping Linn. A *coup d'état* was being planned—so the report had come to him upon his arrival in the city only a few hours before—the object of which was to proclaim him Lord Leader.

On his arrival at the palace of the Patron Saronatt, where the conspirators had set up their headquarters, Clane called the leaders to one of the three apartments that were immediately assigned to him. From the beginning, his attitude was under attack. He listened, startled, as former staunch supporters of his assailed his stand in language more violent than any he had ever had used against him. There were sneers and furious tirades. His fear of an alien invasion, when not openly derided, was attacked on the grounds that only as Lord Leader would he be in a position to defend the state. The arguments were much the same as Czinczar's and were held with equal determination.

Shortly after 3 A.M., a famous Patron denounced his leadership. "I have been invited," he said savagely, "to join the Lilidel group and I shall accept. I'm through with this cautious coward." That was the beginning. The scramble to desert a sinking ship started then. At four o'clock, when Clane started to speak, his audience had dwindled to a score of men, mostly military leaders who had fought with him against Czinczar. And even they, he saw, were not too friendly. For their benefit, he discussed briefly and austerely the possible nature of the coming Riss attack. He did not tell them what his plans were, but he did offer them an emotional satisfaction.

"Our opponents," he said, "do not, in my opinion, realize as yet what they are doing in promoting this particular mother's boy to the rank of Lord Adviser. Children are concerned with the people around them, not with the individuals whom they never meet. Just imagine a child that is now in a position to get its own willful way *every* time." He stood up, and looked around the little group grimly. He said, "I leave this thought with you."

He returned to his own residence, more shaken by the trend of events than he cared to admit. He was on his way to his bedroom when he was reminded by his guards' captain of the assassin.

Clane hesitated. He was tired, and sick of problems. He was not even sure that he was interested in finding out who wanted him dead. Even some of his old supporters might now feel that he was dangerous to them alive. What decided him in the end was his general attitude of curiosity. He attributed his larger success to a habit of quick and thorough investigation of anything that seemed to affect his interest. He ordered the girl brought before him.

She came into the room boldly, spurning the attempt of the guards to lead her in like a prisoner. Seen in the bright light of the oil lamps, she looked older than his earlier impression of her had indicated. He guessed that she was twenty-two or three, or even twenty-five. She was beautiful, by his standards. Her features had the even lines of good looks and keen intelligence. The effect was marred only by the unmistakable insolence of her expression. But he realized that was not necessarily a fault. It was she who spoke first.

"If you think," she said, "that I am the usual type of assassin, you are quite mistaken."

Clane bowed ironically. "I am sure," he said, "that all assassins are unusual."

"I shot at you to attract your attention," she said.

Clane thought back to the moment of the attack. The arrow as he remembered it, had swished by about a foot from his head. For a skilled archer it was a bad shot. The question was, how skillful was she? And how much had the darkness affected her aim. The woman spoke again.

"I belong to the Martian Generals' Archery Club, and two weeks before Czinczar's attack I was runner-up in the championship matches. That's what decided me to take the risk. I was sure I could prove to you that I could have hit you."

Clane said satirically, "Couldn't you have chosen some other method of attracting my attention?"

"No," she flashed, "if I expected to hold it."

Clane stiffened. This was verbal byplay, and he was not interested. "I'm afraid this is beyond me," he said. "And I'm afraid, too, that we will have to follow a more orthodox method of questioning, and assume the usual reasons for the attack."

He paused, curious in spite of himself. "Just why did you want to attract my attention?"

"I want to marry you," she said.

Clane, who had been standing, walked to a chair and sat down. There was a long silence.

He stared at her with bright eyes that concealed more turmoil than he cared to admit even to himself. He hadn't expected to have his hard crust of worldliness penetrated. He had the distinct and unhappy feeling that if he spoke his voice would tremble. And yet it was natural that he should have a strong reaction.

This young woman belonged to a part of Linn that he had considered forever beyond his reach. She was a part of the society that, except for a few men, had ignored the mutation member of the family of the late Lord Leader Linn. The fact that a girl of her station had decided to try to marry him merely proved that she saw him as a way to power for herself. If the night just passed was evidence, then that might be an error of judgment on her part. But her action was the first break in the dike of social opposition. Politically speaking, she could be very valuable to him.

Clane groaned inwardly as he realized that once more he was evaluating a situation in terms of its advantages to his purposes. He sighed, and made up his mind. He called to the guards' captain, "You will assign an apartment to the Lady Madelina Corgay. She will be our guest until further notice. See to it that she is well protected."

With that, he went to bed. He left instructions as to when he should be roused, and lay awake for a while turning over in his mind his plans for the day. Over and above everything else was the visit he wanted to make to the Central Palace to have another look at the monster that Czinczar had brought to Earth.

It would be important that somebody know something about the physical side of man's deadly enemy.

IX

LORD CLANE awoke about midmorning to the sound o
distant singing. It puzzled him for a moment, and then h
remembered that today the Lord Adviser Calaj was arriving
and that a fete had been proclaimed.

He ate a hasty breakfast, and then set out for the Centra
Palace in a patrol boat. As they started to float down for
landing, the pilot sent back a message with one of the guards

"Your excellency, the Square is filled with people."

Clane ordered, "Land on a side street, and we'll wal
the rest of the way."

They landed without incident, and wound their wa
among the dancers and the musicians. They passed swayin
groups of singing men and women; and Clane, who ha
never failed to marvel at the antics of human beings, ob
served them in genuine wonder.

They were celebrating the accession to power of a yout
whom they did not know. Sweet voices, raucous voices, good
natured yelling, women wiggling their hips coquettishly
men snatching at bare arms, kissing any pair of feminine lip
that happened to be passing—it was in its own way
fascinating show. But in view of the danger that had been s
narrowly averted, and of the impending invasion, it was
scene that had implications of disaster.

Physically grown men and women were acting like childre
accepting as their ruler a boy whose only apparent qualif
cation was that he was the son of the great Lord Jerri
Here was so great a love of the childish things of life that a
human life was imperiled.

His thought reached that point—and was violently inte
rupted. "It's that dastardly little priest!" a voice shouted.

The words were flung back among the crowd. There we

angry cries of "Evil One!" "Mutation!" "Devil Priest!" The dancing in the near distance came to a stop, and there was a sullen surging of a mass of people to get nearer to him. Somebody yelled, "It's Lord Clane, the man responsible for all our troubles."

A furious murmur swept the throng. Beside Clane, the guards' captain quietly motioned to the two dozen guards. The powerful men pressed forward, hands on swords and daggers. Clane, who had been watching the incident develop, stepped forward, a twisted smile on his lips. He raised his arm, and for just a moment received the silence he wanted. He called out in his most resonant voice, "Long live the new Lord Adviser Calaj."

With that, he reached into a pouch, which he had carried for years for just such a moment as this, and brought it out clutching a handful of silver coins. With a flick of his wrist he tossed the money up into the air. The metal glinted in the sun, and came down over a wide area about twenty feet away. Even before it landed another handful sparkled in the air in the opposite direction.

Once more, he called, more cynically this time, "Long live the Lord Adviser Calaj."

The crowd wasn't listening. There were shrieks as people stampeded after the money. Even after Clane's party was clear of the danger, he could hear cries of, "Give it to me, it's mine!" "You wretch, you stepped on my hand!" Feet scuffled, fists smacked audibly on the morning air.

The incident made him bitter. Once again, he had been forced to rely on a technique for handling masses of people. Simple, effective, cunning, it was a part of the vast fund of information he had about the man in the street.

In spite of his tremendous desire to dissociate himself from such cheap trickeries, he couldn't do it. He recalled what Czinczar had said. He shook his head. There must be some way of arousing people to the fact that this was the eleventh hour of man's destiny. And that for once all men must put aside personal ambition and act in unison against an enemy so ferocious that he refused even to communicate with human beings.

But how? What could he say or do that would strike the vital spark? He who was spending *his* time and energy study-

ing the machines aboard the Riss battleship, a task so coloss
and so important that all else paled into insignificance besid
it?

Yet here he was, on his way to the palace to do personall
what should have been a routine job for one or more sub
ordinates. It wasn't, of course. No one else was qualified fo
either of the two tasks that had to be done, the political an
the scientific. A few years before, he had belatedly starte
an advanced school for science students; but he'd bee
too busy to give it proper attention. Politics. Wars. Intrigu
People to see. Spy reports to study. Property managemen
Exploration. Experiments. New ideas. Each twenty-four hou
had gone by like a flash, leaving an ever-accumulatin
variety of things to attend to. One man could do only s
much. And now that the crisis was here, he felt the reality o
that.

He was still thinking about it when he arrived at tl
palace gate. The time he noted with automatic attention t
detail, was a few minutes before noon. The question in b
mind was, would he be allowed inside?

It turned out not to be a problem at all. A distracte
captain of the guard admitted him and his staff. Clar
headed straight for the refrigeration room. He had no dif
culty in finding the body of the dead Riss which Czincz
had brought with him from Europa.

The elongated body of the unhuman creature did not a
kindly to the thawing. As the water began to drip from tl
brown-stained, leathery folds of its skin, an unwholeson
stench rose from it. In the beginning, the odor was faint. B
it grew stronger.

As the butchers he had brought along sawed it in
sections, Clane took the pieces and dictated first to one, th
to another of his two secretaries. When he was finished wi
a segment, he handed it to an artist, who drew a lifeli
picture of it with sure, rapid strokes.

As the afternoon waned, the odor thickened until
seemed to permeate every crevice of the room. And st
Clane examined and dictated, examined and dictated. C
flames and test tubes were brought into action. Juices fr
glands, liquid from the circulatory system of the thing, a
fluid from the spinal column were tested with various chen

cals, separated into their components, described, named and illustrated for future reference.

Once, when he put his fingers into a sticky goo and tasted it, one of the secretaries fainted. Another time he tried to feed a piece of it to a rat in a cage. The animal, purposely kept hungry, pounced on it—and died a few minutes later, convulsively.

Clane dictated: "The flesh, on examination, proved to be predominantly a complex protein structure, so complex in fact that it seemed doubtful if it would be edible by any animal of Earth origin. Rat, to which it was fed, died in 3.08 minutes."

Shortly after the dinner hour, he had the parts of the body returned to the box and put back into the ice room. The task completed, he hesitated. Because it was only the first of his two purposes. The other one required his knowledge of how to ride roughshod over another's will.

Once again, he was back in the role he hated. And there was no alternative.

He sent his party home, and inquired the way to Calaj's apartment. The official he spoke to recognized him, and put his hands to his head, as he said, "Oh, your excellency, the confusion today is fantastic. We are all worn out."

He quieted long enough to give Clane the directions he desired. There were guards at the entrance of Calaj's apartment, but they sprang to attention when he said, "I am Lord Clane Linn, uncle of the Lord Adviser."

"Shall we announce you, your excellency?" one asked doubtfully.

"No." Clane was cool and positive. "I'll just go in."

He entered.

There was a little alcove, then a large outer room. As he glanced around him curiously, Clane saw Calaj standing on his head beside an open window. He was exhibiting his skill for the benefit of a Martian slave girl. The girl giggled, and then she turned away, and saw Clane. She froze.

She said something, and Calaj came tumbling down out of his upside down pose. He must have heard his mother express fears about Lord Clane, because he turned pale when he saw who it was.

61

"Uncle!" he said. And Clane did not miss the overtones of alarm in the voice. Calaj was hypnotized by his own anxiety.

In a sense the boy's fears were justified. Clane had no time to waste. He had come to the palace with two objectives, and he had brought along his rod of energy for emergencies. One objective—the examination of the Riss—was accomplished. The other depended on Calaj.

Clane felt remorseless. According to the reports of his spies, this boy was abnormal. If that was so, then he could not be saved. Often in the past, Clane had taken children and grown-ups to a private asylum, and there with all his knowledge had tried to untangle their minds. In vain.

This was no time to hope for success, where so often he had failed before.

Calaj had to be sacrificed. And Lilidel. And all that group behind her.

Destroyed by the madman they had raised to power.

"My boy," said Clane, "I have received instructions from the gods about you. They love you—but you must do their will."

"They love *me*?" said Calaj. His eyes were wide.

"They love you," said Clane firmly. "Why else do you think you were allowed to attain the height of power? Surely, you do not think that any human could have made you Lord Adviser without their permission."

"No, no, of course not."

"Listen carefully," said Clane, "here are *their* instructions for your future actions. Repeat them after me. You must rule in your own right."

"I must rule in my own right." His voice was dull.

"Let no one in the palace advise you on affairs of state. Whatever you decide will be as the decision of the gods."

Calaj repeated the words with a rising inflection. And then he blinked. "Not even mother?" he asked, amazed.

"Especially not mother," said Clane.

He went on, "You will need new people around you. Be careful for a while, but gradually appoint men of your own choice. Disregard those recommended by your mother and her friends. And now, I have a document here—"

62

Arrived at home, he wasted no time. "I am leaving at once," he told the heads of the various departments of his household staff. "You will probably not hear from me for a long time. You will conduct yourselves and the estate as in the past."

The guards' captain said, "What about the assassin?"

Clane hesitated; then, "I suppose the men are expectant?"

"That they are, sir."

Clane said steadily, "I regard this custom of turning a woman assassin over to the soldiery as a barbarous practice, and it will not take place. First, it would be very dangerous for us all since her family is friendly with the new Lord Adviser. You might stress that point to the men, and then say—"

He made his offer of compensation. It was so generous that there was no doubt of it being accepted. He finished, "The offer holds for one year. And captain—"

"Yes, sir?"

Clane parted his lips to make his next announcement, then closed them. It was more than just another move in the complex game he was playing, and yet, the political color was there, too.

I've got to rise above all this pettiness, he told himself. In spite of what Czinczar had said, there was more to statesmanship than animal cunning. It all seemed so obvious; so essential. Because if he also played only the game the others were playing, there would be no hope.

His very determination stiffened him. He said quietly, "You may pass the word along to the company officers that the Lady Madelina Corgay will in future be known as the Lady Madelina Linn. All ranks will treat her accordingly."

"Yes, sir. Congratulations, your excellency."

"The marriage will take place today," Clane finished.

X

"BUT WHAT did you sign?" Lilidel raged. "What was in the document?"

She paced the floor of his apartment in a frenzy of distress. Calaj watched her sullenly, annoyed at her critical attitude. She was the one person who could make him feel like a small boy, and he was silently furious at her for reminding him once again that he should have read what he had signed.

He was not anxious to think about Clane's appearance at the palace five weeks before, and it was annoying that the incident remained as fresh in his mother's mind as the day it had happened. "Why should I read the document?" he protested. "It was just one more paper. You people are always bringing me something to sign; what's one more? And anyway, he's my uncle, and after all, he didn't make any trouble about my becoming Lord Adviser."

"We can't let him get away with it," Lilidel said. "You can just picture him laughing to himself, thinking we're afraid to act against him openly."

That also was the latest of an endless repetition. Psychoneurotic Calaj could not help wondering if his mother was not a little crazy.

Lilidel raged on, "We've sent queries to all the governors, with instructions to scrutinize official documents, with particular emphasis on checking back with us on anything relating to the military establishment.

"Of course"—her tone grew bitter—"asking some of those people to co-operate is like talking to a blank wall. They pay about as much attention to us as if they were the government and we merely hirelings."

Calaj shifted uneasily. His mother's assumption of the word "we" rankled. She had no official position, and yet she acted as if she was the Lord Adviser, and he only her son and heir. He remembered, not for the first time, that Clane had said something about asserting himself. The trouble was, how could he possibly ever dare to oppose his mother and all these dominating people?

It's time I did something, he thought.

Aloud he said, "But what's the good of all this? Our spies report that he isn't at any of his estates." He added, with a sly dig that had become one of his defenses against his mother's dominance, "You'll have to locate him before you do anything against him publicly, and even then I'd hold Traggen in front of me, if I were you. As head of the camp legions, Traggen should do the dangerous work." Calaj stood up. "Well, I think I'll drop over to the games."

He sauntered out.

Lilidel watched him depart uneasily. She was not aware that, in Clane's estimation, her action of poisoning Jerrin had set up conflicts inside her that were not resolvable. But, in spite of the murder, way in the back of her mind, she applied her dead husband's standards of dignity to the great position which Calaj now had.

It had been a tremendous shock to her when Calaj had insisted that the festival celebrating his appointment be extended beyond the three days originally set for it, free to the people, but at colossal expense to the government. The games were still continuing, his interest in them unabated.

Already, there had been even more disturbing incidents. A group of youths, returning with Calaj from the games to the palace, were astounded to hear him suddenly burst out, "I could kill all of you! *Guards, kill them!*" The third time he shrieked the order the nearest guard, a big brute of a man, noticed one of Calaj's companions had his hand on a half-drawn sword. In one synchronized movement, he slashed at the boy with his saber, nearly cutting him in two. In the resulting confusion, nine of the eleven young noblemen were slaughtered. The remaining two escaped by taking to their heels.

Lilidel had had no alternative but to report it as an attempted assassination. At her insistence, the two boys who had escaped were dragged through the streets at the end of hooks, and eventually impaled against the pilings of the river's edge.

Standing there in his apartment—where she had to come these days, if she hoped to see him—Lilidel had the unhappy conviction that what had happened was only the beginning.

During the weeks that followed, she discovered that Traggen had selected several companies of bully boys to act as Calaj's personal guards, and that the men had orders to accept the slightest command given by the Lord Adviser. She could not help suspecting Traggen's motives, but she could find no fault openly with his orders. It was natural that the Lord Adviser Calaj should have automatic obedience to his commands. What was unnatural were the commands that Calaj gave, and all too obviously Traggen the schemer could have no direct control over that.

Month after month, the stories trickled in to her. Hundreds of people were disappearing, never to be heard of again. Their places were swiftly filled by newcomers who knew nothing of what had gone before, or else dismissed as nonsense the vague stories they had heard.

Everywhere in Linn, people in every walk of life intrigued to gain access to the Lord Adviser. The yearning will of thousands of social climbers to become a part of the palace circle was a pressure that never ended. For generations, that had been the road to power and position. But now, success in such a purpose precipitated the individual into a nightmare.

All the trappings and ornamentation that each person's heart craved were there. He attended banquets that consisted almost entirely of out-of-season delicacies, and rare and costly foods from the planets. Each night, the palace ballroom was awhirl with gayly attired dancers. On the surface everything was as it should be.

Usually, the first few incidents failed to alarm the individual. Someone in the crowd would cry out in fear and pain; and it was often difficult to find out what had happened.

Besides, it was happening to someone else. It seemed remote and without personal meaning, and that was true even when it took place close by. The guards—so it was reported to Lilidel—had developed a skillful technique of snatching up the dead body, pressing in close around it, and racing out of the nearest door.

In the beginning it was hard for any particular person to

imagine that such a thing could ever happen to him. But the strain began to tell. No one who was accepted in high government circles dared to withdraw from active social life. But Lilidel began to notice that her listeners were no longer completely sympathetic to her blurred references to the danger of assassination. Too many Linnan families were in mourning for a son or daughter who had been casually killed by Calaj's butchers.

A year and three weeks went by.

One day Lilidel's ceaseless search for a clue to the nature of the document Calaj had signed for Clane was rewarded. A paragraph in a routine letter from a provincial governor was brought to her attention. It read:

"Will you please convey to his excellency, the Lord Adviser, my appreciation of the precautions the government has taken to insure the safety of the populace in the event of another invader bombing our cities. We of Reean, who have before us always the awful example of what happened to our neighbor city of Mura, are perhaps in a better position to understand the practical brilliance of what is being done. In my opinion, more than anything else this has established the reputation of the Lord Adviser among people who formerly might have considered him too young for his high office. The breadth of statesmanship revealed, the firm determination, the break with precedent—as you know farm people are usually the least patriotic and the most commercially minded of the populace in an emergency—are all proof that the new Lord Adviser is a man of remarkable insight and character."

That was all there was, but it was enough for Lilidel. A week of careful inquiry produced the picture of what had happened, and was still happening.

Everywhere except around Linn, city people had been organized and assigned to nearby farms. Until further notice, and under heavy penalties, they were ordered to spend ten percent of their incomes to construct living quarters—and an icehouse for food storage—on the farms to which they were to go if an emergency was proclaimed.

The buildings were to be so constructed that they could be converted into granaries, but for three years they were

67

to remain empty. The city people would do the building, and they were to visit their farm once a month as a group in order to familiarize themselves with the environment.

At the end of three years, the farmer could buy the building at fifty percent of the cost of materials—but with no charge for labor—but he could not tear them down for another ten years. The food in the icehouse remained the property of the city people, but must be disposed of by the end of the fifth year.

Lilidel satisfied herself that this was indeed the result of the document which Calaj had signed for Clane, and then she consulted agricultural experts. They were amazed. One of them said dazedly, "But you don't do that kind of thing to farmers. They won't stand for it. They won't co-operate. And the least we can do now is to *give* them the buildings at the end of the three years."

Lilidel was about to agree with the indictment of the plan when she remembered—it kept slipping her mind—that Calaj was supposed to have sponsored it.

"Nonsense!" she brushed aside the objections. "We will proceed exactly as we have in the past."

She added, "And, of course, we will now extend it to include the city Linn."

She told Calaj afterwards, triumphantly, "The beauty of it is that Lord Clane has actually strengthened your position." She hesitated. There was one thing wrong with her victory. After more than a year there was still no sign of the mutation. He had vanished as completely as if he had died and been buried. Victory—when the loser did not know you had won—lacked savor.

"But what's all this about?" Calaj asked peevishly. "What are the precautions against?"

"Oh, there was some invading ship here from one of the little known outer planets. Your father worried a great deal about it, but when the fleet attacked they had little or no trouble driving it away. I suppose we should have pursued them and declared war, but you can't be fighting the barbarians all the time. The important thing is not the precaution but that the people seem to approve of them. And they think you're responsible."

Calaj said, "But I only signed one paper." It was a point
68

that had been bothering him for some time in a curious irksome fashion.

His mother stared at him, baffled. She sometimes had difficulty following her son's associations. "What do you mean?"

Calaj shrugged. "The reports say that official orders were posted up in every district with my name and seal signed to them. But I only signed one."

Lilidel was white. "Forgeries," she whispered. "Why, if they can do that—" She broke off. "Come to think of it, the one sent us did look odd."

Trembling, she sent for it, and presently they were bending over the document. "It's my signature all right," said Calaj. "And that's the seal."

"And there were hundreds like this," whispered Lilidel, overwhelmed.

She had never before seen a photostat.

A week later, she was still undecided as to whether she should feel satisfied or dissatisfied about the situation when a terrible report reached her. Hundreds of gigantic space ships were hovering over the mountain areas of Earth. From each one of them thousands of monsters were being landed.

The Riss had arrived.

XI

Lord Clane was very much alive indeed. At the appointed hour, more than a year before, he had sent a peremptory order to all sections of the giant ship, and then settled himself at the controls.

The *Solar Star* began to lift. The initial movement was normal enough, but the difference showed within a few minutes. It grew dark with extreme rapidity. The accelera-

tion made the men in the control room look at each othe
with sickly grins.

Clane noticed the reaction, but he stayed on his couch
beside the touch controls. He had a hollow feeling at the pi
of his stomach, but only he knew their destination.

After three hours he reduced that tensing acceleration t
one gravity, and went up to his own apartment for dinner
Conscious of the difficulties that thousands of people ii
the decks below would have in preparing their meals, he
waited an hour and a half before again applying acceleration

Five hours ticked by before once more he reduced the
acceleration to one gravity, and allowed another hour and
half for the preparation and consumption of food. The nex
period of acceleration was four hours. At that time he re
duced the tremendous pressure briefly while his new in
structions were circulated.

"The people aboard this ship," he ordered, "will now sleep
for seven hours. Acceleration will be somewhat greater than
normal but not so great as it has been. Be sure and take ad
vantage of the opportunity."

For the first time then he allowed his officers to transmi
the pattern of travel to their subordinates, and so on through
the ship: "Two (breakfast), three (acceleration), one an
one half (dinner), five (acceleration), one and one hal
(supper), four (acceleration), seven (sleep)." The extra tim
for breakfast allowed for dressing and toilette.

"This," said Madelina, "is silly."

Clane studied her as she sat across the breakfast table from
him. It was their fourth morning of living in the spaceship. H
had wondered how the pressure of acceleration, and th
dreary routine would affect her. For several meal period
now, he had been finding out. As a wife, Madelina was a
outspoken as she had been while a captive. It was time sh
found out the truth.

She looked at him now, her dark eyes flashing. "I see n
reason whatever," she said, "for us to run away. You've go
to be bold in this world, Clane. Maybe that's why you've neve
got anywhere."

Her casual dismissal of all his achievements started Clane
But there was an even more disturbing implication behin

70

her words. After thirty years of being a free agent, he must now adjust himself to the presence of somebody who could talk to him in this critical but undiscriminating fashion. Most unsatisfactory of all, intellectually, was his own reaction to her presence.

Gratitude! A woman of the Linnan aristocracy had sought him out to marry him. She was little more than a child, impulsive, impatient, undisciplined, lacking the experience and training that alone would give balance to her judgments. But he was grateful to her nonetheless. And anxious. Suppose she grew impatient and decided she had made a mistake. He did not doubt that she would leave him, lightly, disdainfully, perhaps seeking some other protector aboard the ship. Czinczar? It was not a possibility he cared to consider.

It was time she found out that this was not just a flight from Lilidel. He said, "After breakfast, why don't you come up to the control room with me. There's an all glass room next to it from which you can get a wonderful view of the stars."

Madelina shrugged. "I've seen the sun before in space."

It seemed to be a rejection, and Clane wasn't sure whether he should be relieved or unhappy. And then, an hour later, just as he was about to increase the acceleration, she came into the control room.

"Where's this viewing room?" she said cheerfully.

Clane saw several officers look at each other significantly. Silently furious, Clane walked towards her. Her action was inexcusable, since he had told her what the pattern of flight would be.

"This way," he said.

She must have noticed the suppressed anger in his voice. But she merely smiled sweetly, and walked in the direction he indicated. She stopped as she came to the door of the viewing room. He heard the hissing intake of her breath, and then she had moved forward and out of sight. When Clane came to the door, he saw that she was already standing with her face pressed against the transparent wall.

Seemingly inches beyond was the great dark itself. Silently, Clane took up a position beside her. His anger was unabated. For this visit of Madelina's, casually calculated to be annoying, fitted in with all the more foolish things that human beings

71

were doing on Earth on the eve of disaster. Each day that went by, it grew clearer that the interrelationships of human beings was inextricably bound up with the Riss danger itself. It was not two or more, but one complex problem.

With a dark awareness of how intricate was this alien war, Clane waited for Madelina's reaction.

The viewing room was unique from the transparent sections in other parts of the ship in that the "glass" bulged out. From where they stood, it was possible to look both forward and backward. Almost directly behind the ship, a very bright star was visible.

Clane said in a low tone, "Madelina, you've made a fool of me before my own staff, coming up like this."

Madelina did not look around, but her shoulders lifted ever so slightly, defiantly. She said, "I think this whole flight is ridiculous. You men ought to be ashamed of yourselves, running away. Personally, I won't have anything to do with it."

She turned impulsively, but there was an intense expression on her face. "Now, look, Clane," she said, "I'm not going to embarrass you again, so don't worry. You see, I know I'm going to be good for you. You're too careful. You don't realize that life is short, and you've got to cut corners and do things fast and without fear. There's only one thing I'm scared of, and that is that I'll miss something, some experience, some vital part of being alive."

She went on earnestly, "Clane, I tell you this trip is a mistake. We should go back and boldly take up residence on the estate. Certainly, we must take precautions against danger, but even if we do get caught in one of Lilidel's traps I'm ready. I love life, but I'm not going to live it on my knees."

Once more she broke her thought abruptly. "What planet are we going to? Mars, or Venus?"

"Neither."

"One of the moons, perhaps? If it's somewhere interesting, Clane, I might feel less impatient. After all, a girl ought to have a nice honeymoon." She pointed at the bright star behind them. "What planet is that?"

"It's the Sun," said Clane.

He helped her presently to one of the nearby couches, and returned to the control room.

A few minutes later, the *Solar Star* was plunging at

tremendously increased acceleration through a space that grew darker with each passing hour.

It was during the supper hour on the fifth day that Clane was informed that Czinczar desired an audience. He hesitated, fighting an instant impatience. Another human hurdle, and an important one.

"Bring him in," he ordered finally.

The barbarian leader came in thoughtfully and accepted the chair to which Clane motioned him. His face was a study of conflicting emotions, but his voice was steady when he finally spoke.

"You madman!" he said.

Clane smiled. "That's what I thought your reaction would be."

Czinczar brushed aside the remark with an angry gesture. "What's the logic behind such a move?"

"Hope."

The barbarian's lips curled, "You've given up the political control of a planet, the enormous geographical distances of Earth to which men can retreat in case of an emergency—for a dream."

Clane said, "This matter of political control is an obsession with you, Czinczar. In the face of a Riss invasion, it is a meaningless achievement. This is not a problem that will be solved in the solar system."

"Nor by a man whose first thought is to escape from danger into outer space," Czinczar sneered.

Clane smiled again, more grimly this time. "If you knew what plans I have, you would swallow those words."

Czinczar shrugged. "Just where are we going?" he asked at last.

Clane told him, "It's a star I located on an old star map of this part of the galaxy."

Having used those magic words, he had to hold himself calm. "Galaxy," other "stars"—even to him who had discovered so much of the science of the days of old, there were new meanings here, emotional excitements on a level beyond anything he had ever known.

"It's about sixty-five light-years from Sol," he said steadily. He watched Czinczar to see if the fantastic distance he had named had any meaning. But the barbarian seemed to be involved in a mental conflict. He looked up finally, his face twisted.

"Men—out there?" Even after a minute of silence, he sounded astounded.

Clane said earnestly, "I want you to picture the golden age of science, Czinczar. Surely, this idea is not new to you, who brought the first Riss body to Linn. Long ago, man's civilization attained a stature that has never since been equaled. In those marvelous days, ships not only went to other planets, but to other stars.

"Then the aliens came. A bitter war ensued. The civilization of the solar system was virtually buried with the destruction of *all* its cities. But out in space, colonies escaped, and continued to develop scientifically beyond anything now known on Earth."

The young man climbed to his feet. "Your excellency," he said in a formal tone, "in my opinion you have by your actions destroyed the solar system. In leaving the Linnan Empire in the control of a mad youth and his murderess-mother, you have at one stroke handed the fate of the known human race over to a government that will be thrown into confusion at the moment the Riss attack, and will remain in a state of confusion until the end. Your imaginative flight is illogical in the first place because, if other men had found a means of fighting the Riss, they would by this time have contacted the people of Earth."

Clane hesitated; then, "There are several possible answers to that. Colonies don't build interstellar ships. Or if these have, then by the time they developed them they had forgotten that Earth existed. Or at least forgotten where it was in space."

Czinczar controlled himself with a visible effort. "Your excellency," he said, "I urge you to turn back. I also believe in imagination, or I would never have achieved my present position. Nor would I have dared to take the enormous risk of attacking Linn. If I had thought you would make this flight into darkness, I would not have surrendered to you, sphere or no sphere."

Clane said, "Czinczar, you're a great disappointment to me. In a curious—I suppose illogical fashion—I counted on your seeing the importance of forgetting all irrelevant personal ambition. I counted on your denying yourself the pleasure which you obtain from military combat—you have some scheme, I know, of fighting a purely defensive war against the Riss. All that, I say, I expected you to forgo in this crisis. And what do I find?"

He made a movement with his hand that expressed some of his own fury at the petty things that Czinczar had done. "From the beginning you have plotted primarily for personal advantage. You have forced other men to take defensive action against you—"

"The idea being, of course," sneered Czinczar, "that these other individuals were not doing any plotting of their own, and would not have intrigued against each other if I had not come on the scene."

Clane said quietly, "Each man must forget his own schemes, his own desires, for the duration. There can be no exceptions."

Czinczar was cold and contemptuous. "Harping on the same old subject, aren't you? Well, I refuse to talk further to a person who has lost his good sense because of a childish, naïve dream. The able man who abdicates his own ideas betrays himself and his state. He must fight for his own convictions against the firmly held ideas of other men. I am convinced that, having adopted such a juvenile attitude, all your plans are now suspect."

He stalked to the door, turned. "Don't forget, the reason the Riss are attacking the solar system must be because there are a limited number of habitable planets in the area of space that can be reached by their ships. I hope you're sure that *we* will find a habitable planet when we reach our destination about—" He paused, abruptly tense. "How long will it take?"

"Something over a year," said Clane.

Czinczar groaned. "Madness," he muttered. "Utter madness!"

He went out, leaving Clane disturbed and upset. The barbarian leader was unquestionably one of the outstanding military logicians of the age, a bold and careful man who had probably examined the entire Riss situation with a minute attention to detail. No fear of unknown distances would influence his decisions.

And yet, his analysis must be wrong. Czinczar simply did not have the understanding of science that alone made possible a considered judgment. All his courage, his calculated risks, and his military skill would merely delay the enemy, not defeat him.

If the answer was not available out in space, then there was no answer.

XII

A week of routine flight went by. At first Clane held himself aloof from some of the precautions that he would in the past have taken against a man like Czinczar.

"If intrigue is ever going to end," he told himself, not for the first time, "then somebody has to take the first step. You have to show people that you trust them."

One little point jarred on him. During that week, it grew in his mind to uneasy proportions. The point was simple. Czinczar had stated unequivocally that he would not cooperate.

Abruptly, on the sixth day, that recollection broke through Clane's reserve. He began to spy on Czinczar. He was intensely disappointed, though, he realized bitterly, not basically surprised, to discover that massive military preparations were under way in the lower half of the ship.

The discovery depressed Clane because Czinczar clearly counted on his own precautions to prevent any spying. It showed up his ignorance of science. His actual preparations were skillful and bold. He had readied Riss-type explosives he had discovered in one of the holds. Crews with battering-rams had been trained to smash down connecting doors which the explosive failed to shatter. The entire barbarian army—a magnificent array of fighters—was divided into groups of a size more suitable for battle in a confined area.

The date of the attack was set by Czinczar for the sleep period of the eighth "night".

Twelve hours before the attack was scheduled, Clane invited the barbarian leader to come up and inspect Riss weapons. He recognized that he was up to his old tricks. He told himself defensively that what he hoped for could only be achieved gradually. In the meantime he must accept the old environment of human machinations that he knew so well.

There was a delay of several hours, while Czinczar discussed the timing of the invitation with his general staff. Finally, he sent a messenger to Clane accepting the offer. But the attack was not called off.

Czinczar arrived at the appointed time with two engineer officers. He ignored Clane's extended hand, saying curtly, "You surely don't expect me to be friendly to a man who tortured me."

"But didn't kill you," Clane pointed out with a faint smile.

"That," said Czinczar, "is because you hope to make use of my forces. Since that involves my own abilities, I must have a picture of the possibilities of our situation, so that I can start training my men. Let us proceed."

Clane felt vaguely sorry for the great man. He was so obviously unaware of what he was up against.

It emphasized—if emphasis were needed—how little he was qualified to judge the hard realities of the Riss war.

It grew clear from the barbarian's next words that he had specific ideas as to what weapons he wanted to see. He said, "Before coming aboard, I was 'photographed' by a machine. That was subsequently done to everyone. What was the purpose?"

Clane led the way to the special weapon control room, with its huge chairs and oversized equipment. He remained in the background while the barbarian engineers exclaimed over the glittering machines and instruments. Czinczar evidently shared their amazement, for he looked around soberly, and then said, "I can see that the Riss are scientifically our superiors in every department."

Clane said nothing. Weeks ago, that had been his reaction, too. Now, he wasn't so sure. Involuntarily, he glanced down at the floor. It was covered by a finely woven fiber mat. In looking under the mat—as he had done as a matter of course—

77

he had found that once there had been another floor covering, a plastic coating of some kind. It was all gone except for chips and fragments.

His workmen had been unable to remove those pieces. The material defied steel chisels.

To Clane, that suggested this was an old ship. The plastic had deteriorated unevenly over the centuries—*and the Riss didn't know how to replace it.*

There was other evidence. Some of the control switches were dummies. In tracing their leads, he had come to empty rooms which looked as if they had once contained machines.

The implications were titanic. The Riss, too, had an unbalanced civilization. More fortunate than man, they had been able to continue to build interstellar ships. Or perhaps they were actually using ships that had fought in the deadly war fifty centuries ago, and simply did not know how to rebuild some of the machines in them.

That gave Clane his picture. Two races struggling up out of the abysmal night, with the Riss far in the lead in the race for scientific advantage.

As of now, their advantage was overwhelming. Man would go down in the first major engagement.

Czinczar was speaking again. "I expect you to stop me if I do anything wrong."

He seemed to have forgotten the protector "photographing" machine. He settled himself in one after the other of the huge control chairs, and began to manipulate dials. With each move he asked questions, while the engineers took notes. "What does this do? And this? And this?" He listened intently, and the answer never seemed too detailed for him. Several times, in spite of extensive explanation, he shook his head and frankly admitted, "I don't understand how that works."

Clane refrained from making an even more extensive admission. He had taken most of these machines apart, and put them together again. But just how they worked was a problem on a different level of understanding. He had made attempts to duplicate apparently simple looking plates and circuits, with completely negative results.

Fortunately, the great ship's storerooms were packed with duplicates, so extensive experiments were still possible.

Czinczar was beginning to understand purposes now. His

gaze moved quickly along the tremendous instrument board; and it was not surprising that he walked over to the "protector" machine, and stared down at it. At this control end, it bore no resemblance to the telescopic "photographic" machine, which had taken his "picture". Obviously, he stared down at the array of locks that were rigidly clamped over every dial.

Clane came forward. "This is it," he said.

Clane began by giving some idea of the intricate science involved, and of the advanced mechanical arrangement.

"As you may or may not know," he said, "the ninety-odd chemical elements in the periodic system are made of atoms, which in turn are complex structures involving nuclei and orbital particles. The outer particle 'ring' of each atom is of first importance in any chemical reaction. Where the outer 'rings' of two elements are very similar, it is difficult to separate them chemically.

"Naturally, clusters of such atoms are in a state of turmoil. They send out a constant barrage of radiation on different energy levels. It would seem at first thought that at each particle level, the radiation of one object would be exactly similar to the same energy radiation from another body. According to the Riss diagrams I have examined—and there are some very interesting films aboard to illustrate the text—these radiations differ on a basis of spacing and timing. They exist in a different space-time. I confess that's been a hard formulation for me to grasp."

He paused. It was the first time he had talked of this to anyone; and he was conscious of a tension of excitement inside him. Sometimes, when he thought of the colossal treasure-house of science he had captured along with the Riss ship, the emotional impact threatened to overwhelm him. That was the feeling he had to fight now. He went on finally, huskily, "This machine"—he pointed at the "protector" instrument board—"sends out a stream of radiation, which permeates the space-time in and around the ship. The radiation runs up and down the scale of energy several hundred thousand times a second. Whenever it resonates—that is, enters the space-time of some other radiation—the temperature of the affected object goes up. This happens to all except 'protected' atoms.

"The nature of the 'protection' is basically simple. When you were photographed, a pattern was set up in a series of tubes here, whereby your position in space was thereafter recognized. This recognition could be used either to single you out for destruction from among billions of other objects, or it could be used to 'protect' you. As of this moment, the radiation skips over you and me and the other people in this ship. It skips over every object in the ship by the process of recognizing them and rejecting them several hundred thousand times a second."

Clane finished, "This is one of the most deadly weapons invented for use against flesh and blood creatures. If I had known they had something like this aboard, I would not have considered making an attack. Every man in the spaceships that took part in the battle was killed. Not just a percentage of them, but every single Linnan in the part of the fleet that actually attacked. My men and I escaped because the Riss patrol boat we were in had a 'protector' camera aboard, which automatically 'photographed' us. Apparently, they used it so that the liftboats could bring specimens to the ship."

The account completed, he waited. He was not too surprised at the prolonged silence. Finally, Czinczar said, "Does it operate only against living matter?"

"It's set that way."

"But it could be used against inanimate objects? You either deliberately or unconsciously implied that in your use of such words as 'object'."

Clane hesitated. Not for the first time, he was startled at the discernment of the barbarian leader. He shrugged finally, and admitted the fact. "Frankly, I don't quite see how it can effectively be used against inorganic matter. It raises the temperature of the entire affected area about sixty degrees. That's fatal for life organisms, but even a tree would survive it."

"You would say then that this instrument could not destroy our planet?"

"I don't see how."

"That," said Czinczar, "is what I wanted to know."

His tone indicated that he had guessed the purpose of the long explanation. His eyes met Clane's, and there was a sardonic light in them.

"You'll have to try again," he said. "I don't scare easily."

He seemed dissatisfied with the limitations of his rebuttal. For he hesitated, glanced at his engineers, parted his lips to speak, and then apparently changed his mind. Silently, he settled himself into the next chair, and began to manipulate the dials of the weapon controlled from it.

Clane held back his disappointment. He intended to come back to the matter, and he had a feeling that Czinczar did too. While he waited, he explained the new weapon.

It operated on a molecular level. It was definitely not radioactive. It seemed to set up a terrific agitation in the molecules of an object. Result: the object burned with a blue-white heat, dissolving quickly into its component gases. It could be used against organic or inorganic matter, but it was a limited weapon in that it had to be aimed and held briefly on its target. He had still to find out if it could be used automatically.

Clane continued, "I've merely tested it. I haven't had time to examine it." He paused ever so briefly, then finished deliberately, "I gave most of my attention to the 'protector' device. Its existence nullifies everything we've got."

Czinczar said quickly, "And the sphere nullifies it."

He looked around, and squarely met Clane's determined gaze. "Think, your excellency, if they try to land, the sphere not only decimates them; it destroys every single Riss in the vicinity."

"All they have to do," said Clane bleakly, "is fly low over one of our cities with this 'protector' device on, and every person in that city dies. A hundred ships could wipe out the population of Earth in a given time."

Czinczar was facing him now. "Then why did they use atomic bombs against the cities they destroyed?" His tone challenged Clane to give a logical answer.

Clane said slowly, "I think it's a weapon they developed since the war that originally destroyed man's civilization. I don't think they wanted us to find out about it from an exploring ship. Its potentialities can be partially nullified by evacuating cities and scattering the population."

Czinczar shook his head. "Your answer is not complete enough. An irresistible weapon doesn't have to be concealed.

You say you've tested it. Knowing your thoroughness I'm going to guess that you know its range."

"About two and a half miles," said Clane without hesitation.

"Since it has a range," said Czinczar, "it obviously must be more effective at one mile than at two."

Clane nodded. "The nearer to the ship the higher the temperature it produces. At two and a half miles it is still fatal, but the individual may be in agony for several hours before death comes."

"What happens when a barrier is placed between it and its intended victims?"

"The men in the Linnan fleet," said Clane, "were protected by several inches of metal, but every one of them died."

"According to your account," flashed Czinczar, "they should have died when they were still more than two miles from the invader. Actually, all of them got close enough for them to ram the big ship. If the ship had been out of control for the full two miles, only a few of them would have reached their objective."

Clane said irritably, "All right, suppose a small portion of the population successfully burrows out of reach of this weapon. A thousand or ten thousand people survive to fight on. Surely, that is not a satisfactory solution. The Riss could ignore them almost completely."

Czinczar climbed to his feet. "Your excellency," he said angrily, "it is clear that you and I do not understand each other."

To Clane, something else was clear. The argument had reached a critical stage.

"Your excellency," Czinczar began, "I am predominantly a military man, you are a scientist. To me, your fear that people may be killed has little or no meaning. People are always being killed, if not in wars, then by other methods. But the wars are ever present, so we need look no further."

He went on grimly, "It is the essential nature of a military man that he must think in terms of percentage losses. Only the skillful leaders must be protected. During a war the death of a first-class military strategist can be a national disaster. The resulting defeat may mean slavery by one means or another for the entire population. In an alien war it can mean the extermination of the race."

Clane parted his lips at that point to interrupt, changed his mind, and then thought better of that, and said dryly, "And who shall decide on the importance of the man? He himself?" He broke off. "Go on," he urged.

Czinczar shrugged angrily. "In certain rigid governmental structures, a single man may lose every battle and still remain in power. But a brave and determined general with enough supporters can break through such an egocentric pattern, and seize control of the defense forces. That situation existed in Linn for one person—yourself." Contemptuously, "You lost your nerve."

"Proceed," said Clane coolly.

"The importance of the leader," said Czinczar, "constitutes one principle of warfare. Another one, even more basic, is that you do not surrender your land to the invader except for specific military purposes, and in the belief that you are actually strengthening your position. Usually, you make him pay a price for it."

Clane said, "If we exchanged one man for two Riss, we would exterminate ourselves, and the natural increase on one or two Riss planets would make up the Riss losses in a single year. Actually, at a conservative estimate, we would lose ten of our own people for every Riss we killed."

"You can't prove that," Czinczar snapped. He waved a hand in annoyance. "Never mind." He went on, "You are wrong in believing that I oppose such a journey as this. But I believe it's too soon. The solar system must be defended first. We must show these aliens that they cannot make a successful landing on any of our planets. Later, when we have established our lines of defense, when we know where and under what terms we can fight, when the populace is trained to the conditions under which the battle must be waged, then and only then can we trust other individuals to carry on."

His eyes were glowing, his face was set in hard lines, his lips tightly drawn together. "There," he said, "you have my argument."

He sat down, and gazed at Clane expectantly. The latter hesitated. So far as he could see, nothing new or important had been brought out. He had considered every one of Czinczar's points long ago, and found them inadequate to the situation. He said finally, slowly, "In the first place, I reject the notion that one or two men are indispensable to the human race, even if they have managed by political cunning to convince a large following that the group can obtain power through them. I have personally told many individuals how I think a war against the Riss would have to be fought. In a crisis, these gentlemen will make their counsel felt."

"Too late," interjected Czinczar.

Clane went on, "This war between Riss and human cannot be won by making a stand on a single planet, or in a single sun system. I am not even sure that an attempt should be made to win it. There you have my second point."

Czinczar said, "I am a great proponent of the limited objective—provided the enemy concurs."

"Thirdly," said Clane, "we will not operate on the basis that half the population, or three quarters of it, is expandable. Leaders with such notions are criminally irresponsible."

Czinczar laughed, harshly. "A good military man accepts the potentialities of his situation. He makes what sacrifices are necessary. Since the alternative in this situation is utter disaster, then the sacrifice of three quarters *or more* of the population is not something that is in the control of the individual leader."

Clane said, "I am sure that I can trust even Lilidel to maintain herself within those elastic limitations. And now"—his tone changed—"before I make my fourth point, I want you to examine this part of the weapon control board." He indicated a section which they had not yet inspected.

Czinczar gave him a sharp look, and then settled down into one of the chairs. His first touch on a dial brought a picture onto a large screen on the wall in front of him. He frowned at a scene in space.

"A window?" he asked doubtfully.

Clane urged, "Go on."

The barbarian moved quickly from instrument to instrument. He grew abruptly tense when he came to those that showed the inside of the ship. In silence, he adjusted more dials, and watched the scenes that unfolded on the plates, and listened to the dialogue that came from concealed loud speakers.

People talking—in their rooms, along corridors, in the great community kitchens. Talking, unaware that they were being

84

observed. Those all-seeing viewers peered in at lovers, and at the headquarters of Czinczar in the barbarian section of the ship. They showed the preparations that had been made by the barbarians for their assault. Everywhere, the evidence was brought to light.

At last, he seemed to have enough. He shut off the instrument he had been manipulating, and sat for nearly a minute with his back to Clane. Finally, he stood up, turned, and gazed at Clane with steady eyes. "What is your fourth point?" he asked.

Clane stared at him, suddenly gloomy. Because he was back on the childish level. In spite of his desire to raise the entire undertaking to a plane where it was above politics, above the need for force, inexorably it had sunk to that level. And now, he had no recourse but to act accordingly. He said, "Very simple. We are on our way to another star. In my egocentric fashion, I have somehow entrenched myself in a position of command. So long as I am in that position, the journey continues. If I should find my control seriously threatened, I would be reluctantly compelled to tamper with the 'protective' machine on a level where it might damage any conspirators. Do I make myself clear?"

The barbarian stared at him with icy hostility. "Perfectly," he said.

He turned with a shrug. "Let us proceed with the inspection."

There was no further discussion. So far as Clane was concerned, it was a defeat for both of them.

XIII

ONE YEAR and eighteen days went by. The giant ship approached the end of its journey.

Twin planets, like two large moons, swam in the blackness ahead. It seemed clear from their size and their distance from each other—they looked about the same diameter—that they revolved one around the other, and that the two of them together followed an eccentric orbit around the hot blue star that was their sun.

The *Solar Star* approached them on a line almost equidistant from each planet. Ranking technical officers—both barbarian and Linnan—gathered in the viewing room. From where he stood near Czinczar, Clane could hear the comments.

"Undoubtedly, both have atmospheres."

"I can see continents and oceans on both of them."

"Look, that must be a mountain. See the shadow it casts."

Clane listened silently. Most of the remarks confirmed his own impressions. He had had a few other thoughts that no one had yet mentioned, but they would come to them, he felt sure.

He waited for additional comments, and presently, as he had expected, they came. A man said, "You'd think we'd have caught the glint of a ship before this. There must be a steady stream of traffic between the two planets."

Another man said, "I've been watching the dark areas of the right side of each planet, where it's night now. I have yet to see the lights of a city."

The murmur of conversation ended abruptly. More than a dozen pairs of eyes turned to stare at Clane. The mutation smiled faintly, and turned to Czinczar.

"They're expecting me to guarantee them that we'll find human beings down there," he murmured in a low, amused tone. The barbarian leader shrugged coldly.

Clane faced his mixed, partly hostile staff. "Gentlemen," he said, "consider the following possibilities. Cities are vulnerable to the aliens; therefore there are no cities. It is much too soon to say that there is no periodic traffic between the two planets."

He walked over and made some adjustments on the auxiliary steering gear. The ship began to turn gradually in its course. Unmistakably it headed for the planet that had been to their right a few moments before.

No one made any comment on the choice. One planet of these twins seemed as good as the other—especially as both could be visited in a matter of days by this tremendously swift ship.

The ship entered the atmosphere of Twin One, as someone suggested they call it, at a sedate speed. On Clane's star map, the two planets had names of their own—Outland and Inland—but the mutation did not mention the fact. The machine sped down toward sea level, and gradually straightened its course until it was moving along about three miles above a hilly wilderness that glinted with streams. As far as the eye could see there was forest or green meadow.

The men looked at each other. Clane walked over to Czinczar and, standing beside him, stared somberly down at the virgin land below. Czinczar spoke first, "It's too bad the aliens didn't find this planet. They could have it without a fight."

Clane laughed abruptly. It was a curiously harsh sound, that startled him. "Czinczar," he said after a moment, "there won't be any fight on Earth either unless the inhabitants of Twin One or Twin Two can provide us with superior weapons."

The barbarian said nothing. He must have sensed something of Clane's intense disappointment.

Somebody shouted, "There's a village!"

Clane counted nineteen houses set rather widely apart, and then a sprinkling of houses even farther from each other. About a hundred acres of trees evenly spaced suggested an orchard, and there were fields of green stuff.

He saw no moving dots which, at three miles, was not too surprising. Human beings did not show up well from a height.

They were past. The houses blurred into the mist behind them, but their existence had already communicated a warmth of excitement to the men in the viewing room. A babble of conversation broke out.

Clane said to Czinczar, "Suppose that this planet was inhabited by an agricultural society. With an army no larger than the one abroad, we could take control. Then, even if we failed to find weapons to stop the invaders, we could have a nucleus of civilization here."

Czinczar maintained a sour silence, and the two men stood without speaking for a long moment. Then Clane said, "Let's see what we find below. Everything may be different than it seems to be."

He changed the subject, "How do you think we should approach them?"

They decided to go in force into several villages. There *had* been several but now the largest was composed of twenty-eight houses, with a scattering of others in the vicinity. It was agreed that individual spies could not possibly infiltrate into such small groups. The individual spy was fine for cities like Linn, where foreigners arrived daily from all parts of the solar system. Here, any new man would be regarded as a stranger. There would very likely be language difficulties so serious as to prevent immediate communication.

Only a force large enough to handle opposition or hostility would be in a position to obtain important information.

The decision made, Clane commanded, "Six patrol vessels will leave immediately. Three Europan, three Linnan." He added, "Good luck."

Groups of men had been training for such expeditions for many months.

As Clane watched them prepare to depart, he said, "I would suggest that we all come back here in four hours. At that time we may have a report."

Clane was back in the view room a few minutes before the time set. He arrived in a room that buzzed with excitement, and it took several minutes to realize what had happened. All except one of the patrol commanders had reported back, and something was wrong.

Quickly, he brought order out of chaos. "One by one," he said sharply, "make your reports." He turned to Czinczar "One of your men first." The barbarian nodded to one of his patrol leaders.

The officer began unhappily. "We found everything as might be expected in a small rural community. They were human beings, all right, and they seemed simple enough, very like our own people. As Lord Clane instructed, we took no hostile action, simply came down and looked around. Everybody was friendly. They were no language problems at all, although we did most of the talking at first. As soon as they realized what we wanted, a man and a woman showed us around. The houses were of simple construction, a little better furnished than we might have expected, but no machinery that we could see.

"Here's what we learned. This planet is called Outland, and its companion Inland. One of the women said she had a sister living on Inland, and she admitted that she visited there occasionally, but I couldn't find out where the spaceships took off. The twin planets are very similar, and life is exclusively farm or village. The name Earth, or Linn, or solar system seemed to be completely unfamiliar to them.

"Naturally, we were beginning to relax a bit. You know what our men are like, high-spirited, and with an eye for a good-looking woman."

The man paused; and Clane glanced quickly at Czinczar to see how the leader would respond to that. The ability of the barbarian leader to control his men had always fascinated Clane. Now, as he watched, Czinczar, slowly and deliberately, winked. It was a startling acceptance of a coarse innuendo by a man who was normally without crudeness. But the result was immediately evident. The officer brightened. Enthusiasm came to his voice.

"Roodge," he said, "is quite a man in his own way. He picked up one of the younger women and carried her off into the bushes. She giggled, and didn't make any fuss, so I decided not to interfere."

"What happened then?"

"I watched the reaction of the other people. They were quite unconcerned. Mind you, I should have known that something was wrong when Roodge came back in less than a minute with a funny look on his face. I figured the girl had got away from him, but I said nothing because I didn't want the men laughing at him. And the silly fool didn't help matters any by keeping his mouth shut."

Czinczar was patient. "Go on."

The reporting officer continued in a doleful tone. "We asked more questions. I wondered if they knew about the aliens. When I described them, one of the men said, 'Oh, you mean the Riss.' Just like that. He went on to say that they occasionally traded with the Riss."

Clane broke in. "They trade with them?" he said sharply.

The officer turned to him, glanced back at Czinczar who nodded as much as to say it was all right for him to answer the question, and then faced Clane again. "That's what he

89

said, your excellency. And I'm sure they recognized the description."

Clane was astounded. For a moment, he abandoned his questioning, and paced up and down before the officer. He stopped finally, and gazed at the group as a whole.

"But that would mean," he said in a puzzled voice, "that they've found some method of neutralizing these Riss. Why would the Riss let them alone and yet come to the solar system and refuse even to communicate with human beings there?" He shook his head. "I refuse to believe that they have really solved the problem of Riss aggression. That problem will never be solved by the human beings of one planet alone."

No one said anything. And presently Clane once again faced the patrol commander. "Continue," he said curtly.

"I knew you'd want to question these people personally," said the officer, "so I suggested that a woman and a man come along and have a look at the ship. I figured it'd be better to take them by persuasion than by force, though naturally if the first didn't work, then it'd have to be the other."

"Naturally."

"Well, our guides agreed to come, made no objection, and in fact seemed kind of interested in a childlike way—the way our own people might have been."

"Go on, go on."

"We started up. On the way, Roodge edged over to the woman and before I realized what was up made a pass at her. At least, that's the way I heard it. I didn't see the incident. I heard the uproar. When I looked around, the man and woman were gone."

Clane looked at him blankly for a moment: and then, "How high up were you?" he asked.

"About two miles."

"Did you look down over the edge? Of the patrol boat, I mean."

"Within a few seconds. I thought they might have—jumped."

"Or been pushed?" Czinczar added.

The officer nodded. "Knowing the quick impulses of our simple people, yes, I thought of that."

It seemed to Clane that the remark was well phrased. The "quick" impulses of the simple folk in Czinczar's part of the ship had resulted during the voyage in the murder of twelve hundred and ninety men and three hundred and seventy-two women. In each case Czinczar's judges had sentenced the killer to a hundred lashes to be given at the rate of ten every day for ten days. In the beginning it had seemed to Clane that a few hangings would act as deterrent, but statistics had proved that only three men so whipped had become second offenders. The lashes apparently penetrated deep, but only into the hides of those who received them.

The officer was finishing his account. "Well, that's about all, sir. Except that Roodge admitted to me that his first girl had vanished just like the second."

Each of the other four patrol leaders reported experiences that were similar in substance, varying only in details. All had tried to bring back guests. In two cases the invitations had been rejected, and they had attempted to imprison a man and a woman. One couple had gone up about a mile and then apparently tired of the "game" and vanished. The third officer described how a Roodge-type man of his troop had offended the woman he'd tried to bring. The fourth commander had actually succeeded in getting his "prisoners" aboard. He sounded aggrieved.

"I thought they got themselves lost in the crowd, and my men are still looking for them. But I guess they took one look at the swarm of people in the corridors, and went home."

His words completed the accounts. With only one patrol still to report, the picture seemed fairly complete.

Clane was frowning over the unexplained details when there was a commotion at the door. The sixth patrol commander burst into the room. Even at a distance, he looked pale and agitated.

"Out of the way," he cried to the officers around the door. "Quick, I have important news."

A path was made for him, and he raced along it, and paused in front of Clane. "Excellency," he gasped, "I was questioning the villagers I was assigned to when one of them mentioned that there was a Riss ship like ours—he definitely said like ours—just outside the atmosphere of the other planet. Inland, he called it."

Clane nodded casually. At such moments as this he felt at his best. He walked over to Czinczar, and said, "I think we should disembark all aboard except our fighting crews, landings to be made on the night side in widely separated uninhabited areas. After a year in confined quarters, everybody needs a chance to get down to a planet again."

"What about the Riss ship?" Czinczar asked.

"Nothing. We remain alert, but avoid battle." His eyes flashed with abrupt excitement. He said tensely, "Czinczar, there's something here for us. I foresee difficulties. We've got to make the most sustained and concentrated effort of our existence. I'm going to make a personal investigation of the village life below."

Czinczar was frowning, but he nodded presently. "In connection with being alert," he said, "how about some of my officers staying on duty up here along with your own? There would be a certain rivalry which would make for wakefulness."

The high excitement in Clane died. He studied the barbarian leader thoughtfully. Finally, he nodded. "With certain precautions to prevent any attempt to take over the ship," he said, "that sounds reasonable."

They smiled at each other humorlessly, two men who understood each other.

XIV

THE LANDING was without incident. Clane stepped down to the grass, and paused to take a deep breath of air. It had an ever so slight acrid odor, and he guessed the presence of minute quantities of chlorine. This was unusual, considering that gas's natural proclivity for combining other substances.

It suggested the presence of a natural chlorine-producing chemical process.

What interested him was that the chlorine content might

explain the faint over-all mistiness of the air. It even looked a little green, it seemed to him suddenly.

He laughed, and put it out of his mind.

The first house of the village stood about a hundred yards away. It was a single-story structure, rather sprawling, and made of wood.

His whole being quivered with eagerness. But he held himself calm. He spent the day on a folding chair near the boat. He paid no direct attention to the Outlanders. Whenever he noticed an individual or a group doing anything, he made a note of it in his journal. He established a north-south-east-west orientation for the village, and recorded the comings and goings of the villagers.

The air grew cooler as night drew near, but he merely slipped on a coat and maintained his watch. Lights came on in the houses. They were too bright to be candles or oil lamps, but he couldn't decide from his distance exactly what they were.

Starting about two hours after dark, the lights winked out one by one. Soon, the village was in total darkness. Clane wrote down, "They seem to be unafraid. There's not even a watchman posted."

He tested that. Accompanied by two husky barbarians, he spent two hours wandering among the buildings. The blackness was complete. There was no sound except the pad of their own feet, and the occasional grunt of one of the soldiers. The movements and the sounds didn't seem to disturb the villagers. No one came out to investigate.

Clane retreated at last to the boat, and entered his closed cabin. In bed he read his day's journal, and heard the vague noises of the soldiers bedding down outside in their sleeping bags. And then, as the silence lengthened, he clicked off the boat's electric lights.

He slept uneasily, tensely aware of his purpose and his need, desperate to take action. He awakened at dawn, ate a hasty breakfast, and then once more settled down to observe the passing show. A woman walked by. She gazed stolidly at the men around the boat, giggled as one of the soldiers whistled at her, and then was lost to sight among the trees.

Some men, laughing and talking, went off to the orchard to the north, and picked fruit. Crane could see them on their ladders filling small pails. About noon, struck by a discrepancy in their actions, he left the vicinity of the boat, and moved nearer to them.

His arrival was unfortunately timed. As he came up, the men as of one accord put down their pails, and headed back toward the village.

To his question, one of them replied, "Lunch!"

They all nodded in a friendly fashion, and walked off, leaving Clane alone in the orchard. He strode to the nearest pail, and as he had half expected, it was empty.

All the pails were empty.

The great blue sun was directly overhead. The air was warm and pleasant, but not hot. A mild breeze was blowing, and there was the feel of timeless summer in the quiet peacefulness around him.

But the pails were empty.

Clane spent some forty minutes exploring the orchard. And there was no bin anywhere, no place where the fruit could have been carried. Baffled, he climbed one of the ladders, and carefully filled a pail.

He was wary, though he didn't know what he expected would happen. Nothing happened. The pail held twenty-one of the golden fruits. And that was the trouble. It held them. Clane took the fruit and the container back to the liftboat, set it down on the ground, and began a systematic investigation.

He found nothing unusual. No gadgets, no buttons, no levers, no attachments of any kind. The pail seemed to be an ordinary metal container, and at the moment it contained substantial, non-disappearing fruit. He took up one of the yellow things, and bit into it. It tasted deliciously sweet and juicy, but the flavor was unfamiliar.

He was eating it thoughtfully, when one of the men came for the pail.

"You want the fruit?" the villager asked. He was obviously prepared to have him keep it.

Clane began slowly to take out the fruit, one at a time. As he did so, he studied the other. The fellow was dressed in rough slacks and an open-necked shirt. He was clean-shaven, and he looked washed. He seemed about thirty-five.

Clane paused in his manipulations. "What's your name?" he asked.

The man grinned. "Marden."

"Good name," said Clane.

Marden looked pleased. Then he grew serious. "But I must have the pail," he said. "More picking to do."

Clane took another fruit from the container, then asked deliberately: "Why do you pick fruit?"

Marden shrugged. "Everybody has to do his share."

"Why?"

Marden frowned at Clane. He looked for a moment as if he wasn't sure that he had heard correctly. "That isn't a very smart question," he said at last.

Clane assumed ruefully that the story would now spread that a stupid man from the ship was asking silly questions. It couldn't be helped. "Why," he persisted, "do you feel that you have to work? Why not let others work, and you just lie around."

"And not do my share?" The shock in Marden's tone was unmistakable. His outer defenses were penetrated. "But then I wouldn't have a right to the food."

"Would anyone stop you from eating?"

"N-no."

"Would anyone punish you?"

"Punish?" Marden looked puzzled. His face cleared. "You mean, would anyone be angry with me?"

Clane let that go. He had his man on the run. He was getting a basic philosophy of life here, one so ingrained that the people involved were not even aware that there could be any other attitude.

"Look at me," he said. He pointed up at the ship which was a blur in the sky. "I own part of that."

"You live there?" said Marden.

Clane ignored the misunderstanding. "And look at me down here," he said. "I sit all day in this chair, and do nothing."

"You work with that thing." The villager pointed at Clane's journal lying on the ground.

"That's not work. I do that for my own amusement." Clane was feeling just a little baffled himself. He said hastily. "When I'm hungry, do I do anything myself? No. I have these men bring me something to eat. Isn't that much better than having to do it yourself?"

Marden said, "You went out into the garden, and picked your own fruit."

"I picked *your* fruit," said Clane.

"But you picked it with your own hands," said the man triumphantly.

Clane bit his lip. "I didn't have to do that," he explained patiently. "I was curious about what you did with the fruit you picked."

He kept his voice deliberately casual, as he asked the next question. "What did you do with it?" he said.

Marden seemed puzzled for a moment, and then he nodded his understanding. "You mean the fruit we picked. We sent that to Inland this time." He pointed at the massive planet just coming up over the eastern horizon. "They've had a poor crop in—" He named a locality the name for which Clane didn't catch. Then he nodded with an air of "Is-that-all-you-wanted-to-know?" and picked up the pail.

"Want the rest of this fruit?" he asked.

Clane shook his head.

Marden smiled cheerfully and, pail in hand, walked off briskly. "Got to get to work," he called over his shoulder.

Clane let him go about twenty feet: and then called after him, "Wait a minute!"

He climbed hastily to his feet, and as the wondering Marden turned, he walked over to him. There was something about the way the man was swinging the pail that—

As he came up, he saw that he had not been mistaken. There had been about eight of the fruit in the bottom of the pail. They were gone.

Without another word, Clane returned to his chair.

The afternoon dragged. Clane looked up along the rolling hills to the west with their bright green garments and their endless pink flowers. The scene was idyllic, but he had no patience. He was a man with a purpose; and he was beginning to realize his problem.

There was a solution here; and yet already he had the conviction that the human beings of Outland and Inland were obstacles as great or greater than he had found in Linn.

Unhappily, he bent down and picked a pink flower, one of the scores that grew all around him. Without looking at it, he broke it into little pieces, which he dropped absently to the ground.

A faint odor of chlorine irritated his nostrils. Clane glanced down at the broken pieces of flower, and then sniffed his fingers where the juice had squeezed from the flower's stem.

The chlorine was unmistakably present.

He made a note of it in his journal, stimulated. The potentialities were dazzling, and yet—he shook his head. It was not the answer.

Night came. As soon as the lights were on in all the houses, he ate his own evening meal. And then, accompanied by two of the barbarians, he started his rounds. The first window that he peered in showed nine people sitting around on couches and chairs talking to each other with considerable animation.

It seemed an unusual number of occupants for that house. Clane thought, "Visitors from Inland?" It was not, he realized seriously, impossible.

From where he stood, he was unable to see the source of the room's light. He moved around to the window on the far side. Just for a moment, then, he thought of the light as something that hung down from the ceiling.

His eyes adjusted swiftly to the fantastic reality. There was no cord and no transparent container. This light had no resemblance to the ones aboard the Riss ship.

It hung in midair, and it glowed with a fiery brilliance.

He tried to think of it as an atomic light. But the atomic lights that he had worked with needed containers.

There was nothing like that here. The light hung near the ceiling, a tiny globe of brightness. He guessed its diameter at three inches.

He moved from house to house. In one place a man was reading with the light shining over his shoulder. In another it hovered over a woman who was washing. As he watched, she took the clothes out of the tub, shook the tub as if she was rinsing it, and then a moment later put the clothes back into steaming water.

Clane couldn't be sure, but he suspected that she had emptied the dirty water from the tub, refilled it with scalding water—possibly from a hot spring somewhere—and all in the space of a minute resumed her task.

He couldn't help wondering what she did with the clothing

when she finished. Did she step "through" to where the sun was shining, hang up her clothes, and have them beautifully sun-dried when she woke up in the morning?

He was prepared to believe that that was exactly what would happen.

She seemed in no hurry, so he moved on. He came presently to the home of Marden. He walked to the door slowly, thinking, "These people are friendly, and without guile. They have no government. There's no intrigue. Here, if anywhere, an honest approach will win us what we want."

Oddly, even as he knocked on the door, it seemed to him there was a flaw in his reasoning.

It made him abruptly tense again.

XV

MARDEN OPENED the door. He looked relaxed and easygoing, and there was no doubt about his good nature, for he did not hesitate. He smiled and said in a friendly, half-humorous tone, "Ah, the man who does not work. Come in."

There was a suggestion of tolerant superiority in the comment, but Clane was not offended. He paused in the center of the room, and glanced around expectantly. When he had looked through the window, a woman had been present. Now, there was no sign of her.

From behind him, Marden said, "When my wife heard your knock, she went visiting."

Clane turned. "She knew it was me?" he asked.

Marden nodded, and said, "Naturally." He added, "And, of course, she saw you at the window."

The words were simply spoken, but their frankness was disarmingly devastating. Clane had a momentary picture of himself as these villagers must see him. A slim, priestly peeping Tom who prowled around their homes in the dead of night and who asked stupid questions.

It was not a pleasant picture, and it seemed to him that his best reply was to be equally frank. He said, "Marden, we're puzzled by you people. May I sit down and talk to you?"

Marden silently indicated a chair. Clane sank into it and sat frowning for a moment, organizing his thoughts. He looked up finally.

"We're from Earth," he said. "We're from the planet where all human beings originally came from, including your people."

Marden looked at him. His gaze was polite. He seemed to be saying, "If you say so, that's the way it must have been. I don't have to believe you, of course."

Clane said quietly, "Do you believe that?"

Marden smiled. "Nobody here remembers such a connection; but it may be as you say."

"Do you have a written history?"

The villager hesitated. "It begins about three hundred years ago. Beyond that is blankness."

Clane said, "We're both human beings. We speak the same language. It seems logical, doesn't it?"

Marden said, "Oh, language." He laughed.

Clane studied him, puzzled. He recognized that the villager could not accept an abstract idea which did not fit in with his previous concepts.

Clane said, "This method you have of moving yourself and your goods from Outland to Inland, and anywhere else on either planet—have you always been able to do that?"

"Why, of course. It's the best way."

"How do you do it?"

"Why, we just—" Marden stopped, and a curious blankness came over his face; he finished weakly— "do it."

That was what Clane had thought. Aloud, he said, "Marden, I can't do it, and I'd like to be able to. Can you explain it to me simply?"

The man shook his head. "It's not something you explain. You just do it."

"But when did you learn? How old were you the first time you did it?"

"About nine."

"Why couldn't you do it before then?"

"I was too young. I hadn't had time to learn it."

"Who taught you?"

"Oh, my parents."

"How did they teach you?"

"It wasn't exactly teaching." Marden looked unhappy. "I just did what they did. It's really very simple."

Clane had no doubt of it, since they could all do it, apparently without even thinking about it. He eyed the other anxiously, and realized that he was pressing the man harder than appeared on the surface. Marden had never had thoughts like this before, and he didn't like them.

Hastily, Clane changed the subject. There was a far more vital question to be asked, a question that struck to the very root of all this.

He asked it. "Marden," he said, "why don't the Riss take over the planets Outland and Inland?"

He explained about the attack on Earth, the use of atomic bombs, the refusal to communicate, and the possibility of future danger. As he described what had happened, he watched the villager for reactions. And saw with disappointment that the man was not capable of grasping the picture as a whole.

He had a mental picture then that shook him. Suppose these people had the answer to the Riss menace. Suppose that here on this quiet planet was all that men of Earth would need to win their deadly war.

And couldn't get it because—

Marden said, "The Riss don't bother us. Why should they?"

"There must be a reason for that," said Clane. He continued urgently, "Marden, we've got to find out what that reason is. Even for you, that's important. Something is holding them back. Until you know what it is, you can never really feel secure."

Marden shrugged. He had the bored look of a man who had jumped to a surface conclusion about something that did not fit into his own ideas. He said tolerantly, "You Earth people are not very smart, asking all these silly questions."

And that was actually the end of the interview. Clane remained many minutes longer, but Marden no longer took him seriously. His answers were polite and meaningless.

Yes, they traded with the Riss. It was the natural thing

to do. The twin planets gave them their food surplus, and in return they took what they wanted of the articles aboard the Riss ship. The Riss didn't really have very much that the Outlanders and Inlanders wanted. But there was always something. Little things—like this.

He got up, and brought Clane a machine-made plastic ornament, the figure of an animal. It was cheaply made, worth a few sesterces at most. Clane examined it, nonplussed. He was trying to imagine two planets giving their food surplus to non-humans in return for useless trinkets. It didn't explain why the Riss hadn't taken over the system, but for the first time he could understand the contempt which the aliens must feel for human beings.

He took his leave, finally, conscious that he had ruined himself with Marden, and that his next move must be through someone else.

He radioed Czinczar, requesting him to come down. In spite of his sense of urgency, he cautiously suggested that the barbarian wait until twilight of the following evening. Clane slept somewhat easier that night, but he was awake at dawn. He spent the day in the folding chair, analyzing the possibilities of the situation. It was one of the longest days of his life.

Czinczar came down shortly before dusk. He brought two of his secretaries, and he listened to Clane's account in silence. The mutation was intent, and it was several minutes before he noticed the barbarian leader's satirical expression. Czinczar said, "Your excellency, are you suggesting that we trick this Outlander?"

Clane was still concentrated on his own purposes. He began, "It's a matter of taking into account certain things that have already happened, and the simple character of Mard—"

He stopped. He heard Czinczar say, "Exactly. I approve of your analysis. I think the idea is excellent." Ever so slightly, Clane shook his head, rejecting the cynical overtones of the other's praise. But he was startled, too.

For nearly twenty-four hours he had planned the pattern of this night's interview. And not once had it struck him that he was playing his old, astute role. There was cunning in what he had in mind, based on a sharp understanding of the difficulty of communicating with these Outlanders. Based, also, on his conviction that there was no time to waste.

"Shall we proceed?" asked Czinczar.

Silently, Clane led the way. He decided not to be ashamed of his failure to live up to the ideals which he considered vital to final success. After all, he was operating in a new environment.

But it mustn't happen again.

Marden received them graciously. His eyes widened a little as he heard Czinczar's wonderful golden voice, and thereafter he listened with a profound respect whenever the barbarian leader spoke. The reaction was in line with Clane's thinking. One of his personal problems on Earth had been that he was of slight build, that because of certain mutational differences in his physical structure, he wore the drab concealing clothing of a priest of the atom gods. What strength he showed was intellectual, and that did not impress other people until they realized its implications. Which always took time.

Not once during the entire evening did Marden intimate even indirectly that his interrogator was asking silly questions.

Czinczar began by praising the two planets and their peoples. He called Outland and Inland two examples of Paradise. He eulogized the economic system. The people were wonderful, the most highly civilized he had ever run into. Here things were done as they should be done. Here life was lived as people dreamed of living it. Here was intelligence carried to the uttermost pinnacle of wisdom.

Clane listened gloomily. He had to admit it was well done. Czinczar was talking to the villager as if he was a primitive savage. There appeared to be no doubt of it. The villager was taking in every word of praise with evident delight.

Czinczar said, "We are like children at your feet, Marden, eager to learn, respectful, anxious to begin the long climb to the heights where you and the people of the twin planets live in a glorious harmony. We realize that the goal is possibly unattainable in our own lifetime. But we hope that our children may share the perfection with your children.

"Perhaps you will give us a little of your time this evening, and tell us at your own discretion a little of what you believe in, of the thoughts that go through your mind, the hopes you have. Tell us, do you have a national symbol, a flag, a plant of some kind, a coat of arms?"

He paused, and abruptly sat down on the floor, motioning the two secretaries and Clane to do the same. It was an unrehearsed action, but Clane obliged promptly. Czinczar went on, "While you relax in that chair, Marden, we sit at your feet and listen respectfully."

Marden walked over, and sat down. He shifted uneasily and then, as if he had suddenly come to a decision, leaned back against the cushions. He was obviously embarrassed by the godlike role that had been thrust upon him, but it was apparent that he could see reasons for accepting it.

"I had not thought of this before," he said, "but it is true; I can see that now."

He added, "I do not quite know what you mean by 'flag' or a plant as a national symbol. I can sense part of the idea but—" He hesitated.

Czinczar said, "Do you have seasons?"

"Yes."

"There are times when the trees and plants bloom, and times when the leaves fall off?"

"That happens to some of them."

"Do you have a rainy season?"

"Yes."

"What do you call it?"

"Winter."

"Do you celebrate the coming of the rain?"

Marden's face lighted with understanding. "Oh, no. The ending of it, not the beginning. The appearance of the first chlorodel anywhere on the planets. We have dancing then, and feasting."

Czinczar nodded casually. "Is that an old custom, or a new one?" He added, "All this may seem unimportant to you, but we are so anxious to catch the spirit of your idyllic existence."

"It's a very old custom," said Marden.

He shrugged regretfully. "But we have nothing such as you mentioned. No national symbols."

As the evening progressed, the villager seemed equally unaware that he was actually answering questions. He took the customs for granted. They were not symbols to him. That was the way things *were*. It was all so natural and so universally practiced. The possibility that other peoples might have other customs simply did not penetrate.

And so, it was established beyond reasonable doubt that the Outlander and Inlander symbol of life was the pink chlorine flower, chlorodel. That each year people visited the underground caverns. That they put a little square box on the table when they ate, and tapped on it when they didn't care to eat much. That they had always given their spare food to the Riss.

One point that came out was especially interesting. There were old, buried cities, Marden admitted. Or rather, ruins of cities. It was years since anything of importance had been found in any of them.

Czinczar talked around that cautiously for a few moments, and then looked at Clane questioningly. That too, was part of their previous arrangement. Clane nodded.

The barbarian leader climbed to his feet. He bowed to the villager. "Oh, noble man of Outland, we have a great favor to ask of you. Would you transport us by your wonderful method to such a city on a hemisphere of this planet where the sun is shining?"

"Now?" said Marden. His voice was casual. He didn't sound opposed to the idea.

"We need not stay long. We just wish to look."

Marden stood up. He was frowning thoughtfully. "Let me see—which city? Oh, I know—where the ship is."

Clane had been tensing himself against he knew not what. He was annoyed to realize that he was just a little anxious. And then—

Afterwards, he tried to analyze what happened. There was a flash, a roundness of light. It was gone so swiftly that he couldn't be sure of just what he had seen. And then, all around was the brightness of day. Almost directly overhead hung the blue sun of the twin planets.

They were standing in the middle of a wilderness of broken stones and twisted metal. As far as the eye could see was a growth of shrubbery and trees. As Clane watched—that was his role; to pretend to be a subordinate—Czinczar walked over to a section of concrete piling and kicked at a thick piece of wood that lay on the ground.

The hard boot made a hollow sound in that silence. But

the wood did not budge. It was firmly embedded in the soil.

Czinczar came back to Marden. "Has any digging been done in this or other cities recently?"

Marden looked surprised. "Who would want to dig in such stuff as this?"

"Of course," said Czinczar quickly. He hesitated. He seemed about to say something else, and then in a curious fashion, he stiffened. His head tilted sharply. Clane followed his gaze, and was surprised to see the *Solar Star* overhead.

That is, for a split instant, he thought it was their own ship.

He realized the truth. He said, "The Riss!"

From nearby, Marden said mildly, "Oh, yes, I thought you might be interested in seeing it, which is why I brought you to this city. The Riss were very interested when we told them you were here in a ship like theirs. They decided to come to Outland to have a look. From something I sensed in your attitude—it seemed to me you might like to see their ship first."

There was a moment, then, when even Clane was disconcerted. Czinczar spoke first. He turned calmly to the Outlander. "We accept your judgment about the uselessness of looking further at these ruins. Let's go back to your house."

Clane caught a final glimpse of the Riss battleship. It was disappearing into the mists above the eastern horizon.

He presumed that it was heading unerringly toward the *Solar Star*.

XVI

As HE HAD done for the journey from Marden's house to the ruins of the ancient Outland city, Clane unconsciously tensed himself for the return trip. Once more, there was the flashing ball of light. This time it seemed even briefer than before.

Then he was in Marden's living room. At the door Clane, who was the last to leave the house, paused. He asked, "Marden, I'm curious. Why did you tell the Riss that we were here?"

Marden looked surprised, then the look came into his face. Another foolish question his expression intimated. He said, "Sooner or later, they ask us if anything is happening. Naturally, we tell them."

Clane said: "Do they speak your language, or do you speak theirs?"

The Outlander laughed. "You keep talking about language," he said. He shrugged. "We and the Riss understand each other, that's all."

The others were moving off into the darkness. Czinczar had paused, and was looking back. Clane stayed where he was. "Do you go aboard the Riss ship, or do they come to the ground?" he asked.

He waited stiffly. There was a purpose in his mind that vibrated with cunning. But he was too angry to be ashamed. The Outlanders' action in telling the Riss of the presence of the *Solar Star* had shocked him. It set the pattern now for his deadly plan.

Marden said, "We go aboard. They have some kind of a round thing which they point at us, and then it's safe."

Clane said deliberately, "How many of your people have had this thing pointed at them?"

"Oh, a few hundred." He started to close the door. "Bedtime," he said.

Clane was beginning to cool off. It struck him that the whole problem needed thinking out. Perhaps he was being hasty in judging these people.

It would serve no useful purpose to risk attacking the enemy ship.

He accepted Marden's dismissal. A few minutes later, he was in a liftboat heading back to his own section of the *Solar Star*. Presently, the ship was moving at a sharp slant up the umbral cone of the nightside of Outland.

A messenger arrived from Czinczar's headquarters. "Great Czinczar requests an interview."

Clane said slowly, "Tell his excellency that I should like him to prepare a written interpretation of what we found out from Marden."

He was getting ready for bed some time later when a second messenger arrived with a written request.

Dear Lord Clane:
  It is time to discuss our next move.

                                        Czinczar.

The trouble, Clane thought grimly, was that he had no plans. There was a great secret here; but it was not to be had by any method he could think of. The human beings of the twin planets could possibly save the race. And yet he was already convinced they wouldn't.

They refused to recognize that there was a problem. Pressed too hard, they got angry, the neurotic anger of someone whose basic attitudes are being attacked. Nor was there such a thing as forcing them. Their method of transportation nullified all the old techniques of persuasion by threat and violence. That left cunning.

Which brought him back to his first thought: He had no real plans. He wrote:

Your excellency:
  I should like to sleep over this matter.

                                        Clane.

He sealed it, dismissed the messenger, and went to bed. At first he couldn't sleep. He kept tossing and turning, and once in a long while he dozed, only to jerk awake with a start. His conscience burdened him. Unless he could think of something, the trip was a failure. He was up against the stone wall of one fact. Neither Marden nor his compatriots could even begin to understand what was wanted.

That was especially baffling because, from all indications, they could read minds.

He slept finally. In the morning, he dictated a note to Czinczar:

Your excellency:

My idea is that we should exchange views and information before we meet to discuss future plans.

Clane.

The answer to that was:

Dear Lord Clane:

I have the feeling that you are evading this discussion because you have no plans. However, since the long journey has now been made, let us by all means consider the possibilities. Will you please name for me the actual information which you think we have obtained?

Czinczar.

Dear Czinczar:

The chlorodel is the "national" flower, because it gives off a gas which makes the air unbreathable to the Riss.

The reference to knocking on a little box in the center of the table when they were not hungry probably dates back to the radioactivity period after the great war. The little box was a detector, and many a time they must have gone hungry because the instrument indicated the food was radioactive.

The annual visit to the caverns derives from the same period.

They give the Riss their surplus food without remembering that that must have started as a form of tribute to a conqueror. In this connection, I would say that only certain foods would be usable by the Riss because of their somewhat different chemical make-up.

Clane.

Your excellency:

Do you seriously claim that the chlorodel can create an unbreathable atmosphere for the Riss? Then we have our answer. We need look no further. Let us hurry back to the solar system, and plant this flower until its perfume is diluted in every molecule of the air of every habitable planet or moon.

Czinczar.

Clane sighed when he read that. The problem of the barbarian leader, pragmatist extraordinary, remained as difficult of solution as all the other riddles.

He ate breakfast while he considered his reply. He took the ship down near the atmosphere of the planet, and spent nearly an hour looking for the Riss battleship, without success. By the time he was satisfied that it was not in the vicinity of Marden's village, another note had arrived from Czinczar.

Dear Lord Clane:

Your failure to reply to my last letter indicates that you do not accept the implications of your discovery about the chlorodel. Let us meet at once and discuss this entire problem.

Czinczar.

Clane wrote:

Dear Czinczar:

I am sorry to see you jumping at a solution which can have no meaning in the larger sense. The Riss-human struggle will not be resolved by the use of a defensive gas. If the Riss ever believed that a campaign was under way to poison the atmospheres of planets against them, they would take counter-measures. They could use radioactive poisons on a planetary scale, or some other gas development as inimical to man as the chlorodel seems to be to the Riss.

The fact that long ago the Outland-Inland Twins defended themselves in that way is not conclusive. The Riss could accept isolated activity. This would be especially true during the confusion that existed toward the end of the Riss-human war. By the time they discovered what the people of the Twins had done, the limited character of the action would be evident. The Riss would accordingly be in an exploratory frame of mind. Even as it was, they must have made threats so terrible that a tribute agreement was made.

I repeat, this is not a final answer. Far from it. In my

earnest opinion, it would be the signal for an attempt to destroy the solar system.

Clane.

Dear Lord Clane:

I am astounded by your purely intellectual approach to these matters. We defend our planets by any and every means at our disposal. Let us meet immediately to discuss the only course now open to us: to return to Earth with a shipload of chlorodel plants for replanting.

Czinczar.

Dear Lord Clane:

I have received no answer to my communication delivered three hours ago. Please let me hear from you.

Czinczar.

Dear Lord Clane:

I am amazed that you have failed to reply to my last two notes. I realize of course that you have no answer, because what can our next move possibly be except return to Earth? The alternative would be to continue our blind search through space for another planet inhabited by human beings. Am I right in believing that the star map which brought us to Outland does not show any other stars as having habitable planets?

Czinczar.

Dear Lord Clane:

This situation is now becoming ridiculous. Your failure to reply to my notes is a reflection on our relationship. If you do not answer this letter, I shall refuse to have any further communication with you.

Czinczar.

Lord Clane did not see that note or the previous one until some time later. He was paying another visit to Marden

110

The interview began unsatisfactorily. The place was bad. Marden was busy picking fruit when Clane stopped under the tree where he was working. He looked down, and he was visibly impatient with the "fool" who had been bothering him for so long now.

He said, "The Riss ship waited for about an hour. Then it moved on. I see this pleases you."

It did indeed. Clane said steadily, "After our trouble with the Riss, we have no desire to meet them. In our opinion they would attack us on sight."

Marden kept on picking fruit. "We have had no trouble with the Riss, ever."

Clane said, "Why should you? You give them everything you own."

Marden had evidently been doing some thinking about the previous conversation on that. He said coldly, "We do not keep from others what we do not need ourselves." He spoke tartly.

Clane said serenely, "So long as you keep down your population, learn nothing of science, and pay tribute, you will be left alone. All this, provided the chlorodel does not wither away. At that point, the Riss would land, and you would learn what their friendship was worth."

It was a dangerous comment. He made it because it was time such thoughts were circulated among these people. Nevertheless, Clane quickly changed the subject.

"Why didn't you tell us you could read minds?" he asked.

"You didn't ask," said Marden. "Besides—"

"Besides what?"

"It doesn't work well with you. You people don't think clearly."

"You mean, we think differently?"

Marden dismissed that. "There's only one way to think," he said impatiently. "I find that it's easier to use spoken language with you, and search your minds for the right word when I might otherwise be at a loss. All those who have dealt with you feel the same way." He seemed to think that settled the matter.

Clane said, "You don't really speak our language? You learn it by getting some of our thoughts as we speak?"

"Yes."

Clane nodded. Many things were becoming much clearer. Here was a human colony that had carried on to new heights of scientific development long after the connection between Earth and Outland was broken. The reasons for their subsequent decadence were probably intricate: Disruption of commerce with other man-inhabited planets. Destruction of tens of thousands of their own factories. Irreplaceable gaps in the ranks of their technicians. The deadly pressure of Riss threats. Inexorably, that combination had added up to the present static state.

Clane said, "Does the reading of minds have any relation to your method of transportation?"

Marden sounded surprised. "Why, of course. You learn them at the same time, though it takes longer."

He climbed down from the tree, carrying his pail. "All this time while you've been talking, there's been a question in the back of your mind. It's your main reason for this visit. I can't quite make it out, but if you will ask it, I'll answer as best I can, and then I can go to lunch."

Clane took out his star map. "Have you ever seen one of these?"

Marden smiled. "At night, I look up into the sky, and there it is."

"Apart from that?"

"I have seen occasional thoughts about such maps in the minds of the Riss."

Clane held the map up for him. "Here is your sun," he said. He pointed. Then brought his finger down. "And here is ours. Can you use the knowledge in my mind about such things to orient yourself to this map, and point out to me which is the nearest Riss sun?"

There was a long silence. Marden studied the map. "It's hard," he sighed. "But I think it's this one."

Clane marked it with trembling fingers, then said huskily, "Marden, be as sure as you can. If you're wrong, and we go there, we will have wasted half a year or more. Millions of people may die."

"It's either this one or this one," said Marden. He pointed a star about an inch from the other one.

Clane shook his head. "That one's a hundred light-years, and this one about twenty."

"Then it's the close one. I have no impression of the distance being very great."

"Thank you," said Clane, "I'm sorry to have been such a nuisance."

Marden shrugged.

"Good-by," said Clane.

He turned and headed back to the liftboat.

XVII

BACK ON THE ship, he read Czinczar's letters with an unhappy sense of more trouble to come. He ate lunch, and then, bracing himself invited the angry barbarian for a conference.

He included an apology in his letter. He explained where he had been, though not his purpose in visiting Marden.

That account he saved until Czinczar and he were alone together. When he had finished, the great man sat for a long time saying not a word. He seemed unutterably nonplussed. At last, he said in a mild tone, "You have no faith in the chlorodel plant?"

Clane said, "I see it as a weapon of last resort. We mustn't use it till we are sure we understand all the possible repercussions."

Czinczar sighed. "Your action in producing the chlorodel as a weapon had decided me that this journey was worthwhile after all. Now you yourself devaluate it, and suggest that we extend our trip to take in the planets of another star."

He brought up one hand, as if he would use it somehow to make his protest more effective. He seemed to realize the futility of that, for he spoke again.

"I confess it baffles me. What can you possibly hope to gain by going to a Riss planet?"

Clane said earnestly, "If Marden is right, it would take us

113

three months. Actually, the Riss star is almost, though not quite, as near to Earth as this one." He paused. He was anxious to have moral support for the journey. He went on, "I honestly believe it is our duty to investigate the potentialities of taking counteraction against man's deadly enemy. This war will not be won on the defensive."

He saw that Czinczar was looking straight at him. The barbarian said, "If Marden is right—that's a damning phrase." He shook his head in visible despair. "I give up. Anybody who will order a ship as big and important as this one to make a trip on the strength of Marden's memory of what he saw in the mind of a Riss—"

He broke off. "Surely, there must be maps aboard the *Solar Star*."

Clane hesitated. This was a sore point with him. He said carefully, "We had an unfortunate accident at the time we took over the ship. Everyone was in an exploring frame of mind, and one of the men wandered into the map room. Can you guess the rest?"

"They'd set energy traps for interlopers."

"He was killed, of course," Clane nodded drably. "It was a lesson for us all. I discovered that all the main control and mechanical departments were similarly mined. We used condemned slaves to do the dangerous work, promising them freedom if they were successful. Result: Only one other accident."

"What was that?" asked the ever-curious Czinczar.

"The interstellar television communicator," Clane replied. He broke off. "I regret as much as you do that we have to make our next move on the basis of Marden's memory."

He hesitated, then made his appeal. "Czinczar," he said slowly, "although I have apparently ignored your opinions on this journey, I do have a high respect for them. I sincerely believe you are being too narrowly practical. You are too bound to the solar system. I don't think you realize how much you think of it as a home that must be defended to the death. But never mind that. What I have to say to you is no longer based strictly on logic, or even on whether or not we are in agreement.

"I ask for your support because, first, I am the commander of this ship for better or worse; second, if we do come to a

114

Riss planet I intend us to take enormous risks—and that will require your fullest cooperation; third, in spite of all your doubts, you yourself feel that the discovery of the chlorodel plant partially justifies the journey so far. I disagree with that, but at least it goes to show that there are secrets to be discovered out here."

He finished quietly, "That's all I have to say. What's your answer?"

Czinczar said, "In our correspondence, and in our present discussion, neither you nor I have referred to the Outlander method of transportation. What is your reason for not mentioning it? Don't you think it has any value?"

The very extent of the thoughts he had had on the subject held Clane momentarily silent. He said finally, "It would be a terrific advantage, but I can't see it as being decisive— as it now stands. Besides, we can't get it."

He explained the efforts he had made, and the impossibility of gaining the secret from the mercurial inhabitants. He finished, "I do have a plan about it. My idea is that we leave behind young couples to whom children were born during the trip. Their instructions will be to try to have their youngsters trained by the Outlanders. That will take nine years."

"I see." Czinczar frowned at the floor, finally stood up. "If there's any fighting to do when we get to the Riss planet, call on me. Is that what you mean by support?"

Clane smiled wanly, and also stood up. "I suppose so," he said. "I suppose so."

Lord Clane Linn walked slowly to the weapon control room after separating from Czinczar. For a long time, he sat in one of the giant chairs, idly manipulating a viewing instrument. Finally, he shook his head. The unpleasant fact was that Czinczar's doubts about accepting Marden's directions had convinced him. Such a trip still had to be made, but not on such a flimsy basis.

Unfortunately, the only other idea he had was so wild— and dangerous—he still hadn't mentioned it to anyone. Even Czinczar had not suggested an attack on the other Riss battleship.

Six hours went by. And then a message arrived from the barbarian leader.

Dear Lord Clane:
 The ship is not accelerating. What's the matter? If we are going on this journey, we should be on our way.
Czinczar.

Clane bit his lips over the letter. He did not answer it immediately, but its arrival stiffened him to the need for a decision. *At least*, he thought, *I could go down again, and see Marden.*

It was already dark when he landed in the village. Marden opened the door with the reluctance of a man who knew in advance who his visitor was, and was not interested.

"I thought you were leaving," he said.

"I have a favor to ask," said Clane.

Marden peered through the slit of the door, polite from habit.

"We have to try to come to an agreement with the Riss," said Clane. "Do you think one of your people—of those who are allowed aboard the Riss ship—would be willing to help my emissaries meet the Riss?"

Marden laughed, as at a private joke, "Oh, yes, Guylan would."

"Guylan?"

"When he learned of the enmity between you and the Riss, he thought something should be done to bring you together." Marden's tone suggested that Guylan was a little simple about such things. He finished, "I'll talk to him about this in the morning."

Clane urged, "Why not now?" He had to fight his impatience. "All this is very serious, Marden. If our two ships should meet, there might be a big battle. It's not too late in the evening yet. Could you possibly contact him for me immediately?"

He tried to hide his anxiety. There was just a chance that Marden would realize his real intentions. He was counting on their intricacy, and their mechanical aspects, to baffle the Outlander's suspicions. He saw that the man seemed doubtful.

"There's something about your purpose—" Marden began.

He shook his head. "But then you people don't think straight, do you?" He seemed to be talking to himself, "This fear of yours," he said aloud thoughtfully. Once more he failed to finish a sentence. "Just a minute," he said.

He disappeared into the house. Not one, but several minutes went by. Then he came to the door with a tall, thin, mild-faced man.

"This is Guylan," he said. He added, "Good night." He closed the door.

The battle began in the hours of darkness before the dawn. In the weapon control room, Clane sat in a chair at the back of the room. From that vantage point he could see all the viewing plates.

High on the "forward" screen, the Riss battleship was clearly visible. Like a monstrous torpedo, it was silhouetted against the dark sky of Outland.

All the plates were on infrared light control, and visibility was amazingly sharp.

A hand tugged at Clane's arm. It was Guylan. "Is it time?" the Outlander asked anxiously.

Clane hesitated, and glanced at the thirty volunteers waiting in the corridor outside. They had been training for hours, and there was such a thing as letting too much tension build up. They had their instructions. All he had to do was give the signal.

His hesitation ended. "All right, Guylan," he said.

He did not look to see what the reaction was, but touched a button that flicked on a light in front of the man controlling the molecular weapon. The officer paused to aim along a sighting device, and then released the firing pin.

He held the aiming device steady.

A line of fire crept along the length of the enemy battleship. The effect was beyond Clane's anticipation. The flame licked high and bright. The night came alive with the coruscating fury of that immense fire. The dark land below sparkled with reflected glare.

And still there was no answering fire. Clane stole a glance at the corridor, where the volunteers had waited. It was empty.

A shout brought his gaze back to the Riss ship. "It's falling!" somebody yelled.

It was, slowly and majestically, one end tilted down, and the other end came up. It made a complete somersault in the first five miles of its fall, and then began to spin faster. The man manipulating the screen on which it had been visible lost sight of it for a few seconds. When he brought it into focus again, it was ten miles nearer the ground, and still falling.

It struck the ground with a curious effect. The soil did not seem solid, but acted as a liquid might. The ship went into it for about a third of its length.

That was their only indication of how tremendous the impact had been.

The weapon officers were cheering wildly. Clane said nothing. He was trembling, but mass enthusiasm was something in which he was constitutionally incapable of joining. He caught a movement out of the corner of one eye. He turned. It was Guylan.

The Outlander had a hurt expression on his face. "You didn't play fair," he said, as soon as he could make himself heard. "I thought this was supposed to be an attempt to be friendly."

It was a moment for guilt feelings, a time to think of abandoned ideals. Clane shook his head. He felt sorry for the Outlander, but he was not apologetic. "We had to be prepared for an attack," he said. "You can't fool with beings who bombed Earth cities."

"But it was you who attacked," Guylan protested. "The moment I put your men aboard each one ran for some machine, and exploded something."

"The Riss have other ships," said Clane diplomatically. "Thousands of them. We have only this one. To make them talk to us, we have to get them where they can't get away."

"But they're all dead," Guylan said plaintively. "The fall killed everybody aboard."

Clane tried to hold down his feeling of triumph. "It did strike the ground rather hard," he admitted.

He realized that the conversation was getting nowhere. "See here, Guylan, this whole business is deadly, and you're looking at it from too narrow a viewpoint. We want to make contact with the Riss. So far, they haven't let us. If you'll look into my mind, you'll see that that's true."

Guylan said unhappily after a moment, "I guess that's so

all right, but I didn't realize before what you were going to do. There was something in your mind but—"

Clane could understand a part of the other's dilemma. All his life Guylan had taken for granted that he knew what was going on in other people's minds. But he had not been able to grasp the notion that thirty men could attack a gigantic battleship with tens of thousands of powerful beings aboard. And that that small number of individuals would set off booby traps which the Riss had designed to protect their secrets in the event a ship ever fell into the possession of an enemy. The concept involved mechanical understanding. Accordingly, it was beyond Guylan and his fellows. Lacking the knowledge, lacking the complex associations, their mind-reading ability was of no use to them in this situation.

Clane saw that the man was genuinely dispirited. He said quickly, "Look, Guylan, I want to show you something."

Guylan said glumly, "I think I'd better go home."

"This is important," said Clane. He tugged gently at the other's sleeve. Guylan allowed himself to be led to the "protector" instrument. Clane indicated the main switch. "Did you see one of our men shut this off by pushing it like this?" He grasped the instrument, and plunged it deep into its socket. It locked into position.

Guylan shook his head. "No, I don't remember."

Clane said earnestly, "We've got to make sure of that." He explained how the "protector" worked, and that any Outlander who wandered near the ship would die. "You've got to go aboard, Guylan and shut that off."

Guylan said in surprise, "Is this the thing that they guarded me against, and the others who were allowed aboard?"

"This is it. It kills everything in a two and a half mile range."

Guylan frowned. "Why didn't it kill the the men I took aboard?"

Clane swallowed hard. "Guylan," he said gently, "have you ever seen a man burned alive?"

"I've heard of it."

"Did he die right away?"

"No. He ran around madly."

"Exactly," said Clane grimly. "Guylan, those volunteers started to burn all through their bodies the moment they got

119

aboard. But they didn't die right away. They gambled on getting that machine shut off in time."

It didn't work exactly like that. But it was too difficult to explain what happened to the metabolism of a human being when the temperature in every cell of his body suddenly went up sixty degrees.

The Outlander said uneasily, "I'd better hurry. Somebody might get hurt."

He vanished. That made Clane jump. It was the first time he had actually seen it happen, and it gave him an eerie feeling. Abruptly, Guylan was standing beside him again.

"It's off," he said. He seemed relieved.

Clane held out his hand. "Guylan," he said warmly, "I want to thank you."

The Outlander shook his head. He had evidently been doing some thinking. "No," he said, "that was all unfair. You treated the Riss unfairly." A stubborn expression grew into his mild face. "Don't ever ask me to do you another favor."

"Thank you just the same."

Afterwards, Clane thought, *First, I'll go aboard, and get the maps, and then—*"

He had to struggle against the tremendous excitement that was in him. He pictured the message he would send to Czinczar just before breakfast. Abruptly, he couldn't restrain himself. He sat down, and with quivering hand dashed off the message:

Dear Czinczar:
    You will be happy to know that we have successfully engaged the enemy warship. Our victory includes capture of his ship, and destruction of all Riss aboard. It is interesting to note that captured maps identified the nearest Riss star as the one picked by Marden.

Clane.

As it turned out, the final sentence of the note had to be rewritten before the message was delivered. The captured maps proved that Marden knew nothing about the direction of stars. The Riss sun was about three months away, but in exactly the opposite direction.

By the follow evening, the *Solar Star* was on its way.

XVIII

THE FIRST squall from the boy came faintly to Clane's ears through the thick panels of the bedroom door. The sound of it electrified him. He had already ordered acceleration down to one G. Now, he went to the laboratory that adjoined the control room, intending to work. But a great weariness was upon him. For the first time, he realized how tense he had been, how tired he was. He lay down on the cot and fell asleep immediately.

It was morning when he awakened. He went to Madelina's and his apartment, and at his request the baby was shown to him. He examined it carefully for indications that his own mutational characteristics had been passed on, but there was no sign of anything out of the normal. It baffled him. Not for the first time, he had a sense of frustration. He knew so little in a world where there was so much to know.

He wondered if there might be neural similarities between the child and himself. He hoped so. For he did not doubt his own greatness. His history proved that he was perceptive as few men had ever been. And he was just beginning to suspect that he was also supernormally stable.

He'd have to watch the child for indications that the two of them were—different.

Except for its structural normalcy, the appearance of the baby gave him no aesthetic satisfaction. It was about as ugly a child as he had ever had the misfortune to look upon, and he was startled when the head nurse crooned, "Such a beautiful child."

He supposed that it might turn into one since Madelina was an extremely good-looking girl. And he presumed that the child's normalcy proved that her side of the family would dominate it physically.

Looking down at the child as it was being clothed again after its bath, he grew sad. He had been worried about the possibility of mutational changes and he was happy that there were none. But he could already imagine the boy being ashamed of his father.

That thought ended when a nurse came out of the bedroom and told him that Madelina was awake and was asking for him. He found her cheerful and full of plans.

"You know," she said, "I never before realized what wonderfully considerate people we have with us. The women have been just marvelous to me."

He gazed thoughtfully at her as she talked. During the long voyage, Madelina had undergone profound psychological adjustments. There had been an incident involving an assassin of Lilidel's who had somehow got aboard in the guise of a soldier. The would-be killer never guessed how hopeless his purpose was. On approaching their apartment he set off alarms; and so Clane had deliberately invited Madelina to be in at the death. The man's desperate will to live had affected her tremendously. From that moment, she ceased to talk of death as something she could take or leave alone.

He listened now, happy in the change that had taken place, as she praised several of the servants individually. She broke off abruptly. "Oh, I almost forgot. You know how hard it's been for us to decide on his name—well, I dreamed it: Braden. Just think that over for a minute. Braden Linn."

Clane accepted the name after a moment's hesitation. A child's first name should be individual, to distinguish him from others of his line. There would have to be a string of second names, of course, to honor the famous men of both families. It was an old custom, and one of which he approved, this giving of many family names. It reminded the bearer of the past history of his line. It brought a sense of continuity of life, and gave the proud possessor a feeling of belonging; a will to do as well as, or better, than his namesake. Even he, who had so many physical reasons for not having that sense of belonging, had felt the pressure of the many names that had been bestowed upon him at the hour of his christening.

The full name finally given to the new baby was Braden Jerrin Garlan Joquin Dold Corgay Linn.

It was two weeks after the birth that the *Solar Star* came to its second destination in space.

Clane entered the conference room briskly. Now, at last there was no reason for inner conflicts. An enemy planet was already bright in the darkness ahead of them.

It was time to prepare for action.

First, he made his prepared speech, stressing the value of courage. His eyes studied the faces of the men as he talked, watching for signs of cynicism. He didn't expect too much of that. These were earnest men, conscious of the reality of their mission.

Some of them, he saw, appeared puzzled by the tenor of his talk. There was a time when he would have yielded to that gathering impatience. No more. In every great objective the leader must start from the beginning, first evoking the emotional attitude necessary to success. In the past he'd assumed automatically that soldiers took courage for granted. They did, but only if they were reminded. And even then, on the general staff level, there was resistance from individuals.

Having completed his diatribe on courage, he launched into the explanation of his purpose. He hadn't gone far before he began to notice the reactions.

The officers, barbarians as well as Linnans, were almost uniformly pale. Only Czinczar was frowning with a sudden thoughtful air, his eyes narrowed with calculation.

"But, your excellency," one of the Linnans protested, "this is a major Riss planet. They'll have hundreds of ships to our one."

Clane held himself cool. It was an old experience with him now to realize that only he had reasoned out the situation as a whole. He said gently, "Gentlemen, I hope we are all agreed that this ship and those aboard must take risks to the limits of good sense."

"Yes, but this is madness." It was General Marak, now Clane's private secretary. "As soon as they discover us——" He paused, as if he had been struck by a new thought. He said, "Or do you expect that we will not be discovered?"

Clane smiled. "We'll make sure that we are. My plan is to land most of the"——he hesitated, and bit his lips; he'd almost said "barbarian", then he went on—"Europan army, and establish a bridgehead."

The faces of the barbarian officers took on a sick expression, and almost everyone in the room looked appalled. Once more, the exception was Czinczar. Clane was aware of the barbarian leader watching him with bright eyes, in which the light of understanding was beginning to dawn. Clane stood up.

"Gentlemen," he chided, "you will refrain from frightening the troops with your all too obvious dismay. Our approach to this problem is soundly based. Spaceships are *not* destroyed in space. They cannot even maintain contact with each other when those aboard are friendly to each other, and make every effort to keep together. So you may be sure that the Riss will not contact us as long as we keep moving."

"As for the landing, it is the oldest reality of military history that a bridgehead can always be established and held for a time. And no one has *ever* figured out a method of preventing an enemy from landing somewhere on a planet."

He broke off. "But now, enough of argument. We have our purpose. Now, we come to what is far more important, the intricate details of carrying out that purpose."

He explained his own ideas, and then, before throwing the meeting open to general discussion, finished, "In everything, we must follow the rule of the calculated risk. We must be aware at all times that there will be sacrifices. But in my opinion, no plan can be acceptable which does not offer some hope of saving a fairly large percentage of the bridgehead army."

Czinczar was the first to get up. "What," he asked, "is the exact purpose of the landing?"

"To see what reaction it brings, how strong the reaction is, how they attack, with what weapons? In short, how do the Riss plan to defend their planet?"

"Isn't it possible," Czinczar asked, "that this information was known to the ancient humans who fought the great Riss-human war?"

"Perhaps." Clane hesitated, not sure whether this was the moment to offer his own estimate of that past war, and its conduct. He decided finally that it wasn't. He said, "I found no books on the war itself, so I can't answer your question."

Czinczar looked at him steadily for several seconds, and

then finished, "Naturally, I am in favor of the landing. Here are my ideas on your plan—"

The discussion continued on that practical level. There were no further objections to the landing itself.

XIX

THEY CAME down on the dried out, uneven hillside of what might have been a dead sea. Rock formations tangled that unpleasant and desolate terrain. The air was thin and cold in the morning, but by noon the heat had become a blistering thing.

The men were grumbling even as they set up their tents. Clane was aware of many a scowl sent in his direction as he flew slowly along within a few feet of the ground. And a dozen times when his ship came silently over a rock formation before dipping down into the next valley, he overheard fearful comments from big men whose courage in battle could be counted on.

Periodically, he landed to inspect the protector and molecular energy devices he had ordered set up. The protectors were the same instruments that had killed every man of the skeleton crews aboard the Linnan warships in the attack that had originally enabled him to seize the *Solar Star*. The molecular weapons had burned great gashes in the second Riss ship. He made sure that the destructive limit of each weapon was set at extreme range, and then he flew on.

He stood finally beside Czinczar, gazing out toward the bleak horizon. The barbarian was silent. Clane turned and gave his final instructions.

"Send out raiding-parties. If you get any prisoners, report to me immediately."

Czinczar rubbed his chin. "Suppose they drop atomic bombs on us?"

Clane did not answer at once. From the hillside, he could see some of the tents. Most of them were hidden in the hollows behind crooked rock formations. But here and there he could see the thin, unsteady lines. They reached to the horizon and beyond—over thirty miles in each direction from where they stood.

An atomic bomb would kill everybody in its immediate vicinity. The titan wind would tear down every tent. The radiation, that deadly stuff, would bounce from the hard, glittering rock, and kill only the few man who were directly exposed.

That was for a bomb exploding at ground level. If it exploded in the air, if for instance the automatic controls of the molecular weapons forced it to explode at a height of twenty miles, the effect would be compressive. But at twenty miles the air pressure would not be too deadly, particularly for men who had orders to burrow into the rock under their tents, and *orders* that two of the four men assigned to each tent must always be in the rock burrow. The other two men of each unit were expected to be alert. It was presumed that they would hastily take cover if a Riss ship appeared overhead.

Clane explained his picture, and finished, "If they drop a bomb on us, why, we'll drop one or two on their cities."

His surface coldness yielded to his inner exultation. He laughed softly, and said, "No, no, my friend. I'm beginning to grasp the problem of two hostile civilizations in this vast universe. There's never been anything like it, before human and Riss collided. No planet can be defended. All planets can be attacked; everybody is vulnerable—and this time, here on one of their home planets, we have the least to lose."

He held out his hand. "Good luck to you, Great Czinczar. I'm sure you will do your usual thorough job."

Czinczar gazed down at the proffered hand for several seconds, and finally took it. "You can count on me, sir," he said.

He hesitated. "I'm sorry," he said slowly, "that I didn't give you the sphere."

The frank admission shocked Clane. The loss of the sphere had been a major disaster, and only the terrible will power of the barbarian leader had restrained him finally from forcing the issue to a conclusion. Even then he had realized his need for such a man as Czinczar. He could not bring himself to say that it didn't matter. But since the confession implied that the sphere would be available on Earth, he said nothing.

Back on the *Solar Star*, he guided the ship from the weapon control room. A dozen men stood behind him, watching the various screens, ready to call his attention to any point that he himself might miss.

They cruised over cities—all of them were in mountain areas—and it didn't take very long to discover that they were being evacuated. Endless streams of small craft poured from each metropolitan area, unloaded their burden of refugees, and came back for more.

The spectacle exhilarated the other officers. "By all the atom gods," one man exulted, "we've got those skunks on the run."

Somebody urged, "Let's drop some bombs on them—and watch them scurry."

Clane said nothing, simply shook his head. He was not surprised at the virulence of the hatred. For two days he watched it swell and surge around him, and still it showed no signs of diminishing.

"I've got to change these automatic hate patterns," he told himself. But that was for later.

During those two days, he received periodic radio reports from Czinczar. Patrols had been sent out. That was one message. About half of them were back by the time the second report arrived.

"It appears," said Czinczar, "that an army is gathering around us. There is much activity on every side, and our patrol craft have been burned down by ground artillery at heights as great as eighteen miles. So far there has been no attack made on any of our machines from the air. It looks as if they are trying to contain us. Our men have captured no prisoners as yet."

The third report was brief. "Some air activity. No prisoners. Shall we try to go into one of their camps?"

Clane's answer to that was, "No!"

Seen from a great height, the problem of the Riss planet fascinated him. It seemed clear that a sharp clash was imminent. Considering how many individual Riss there were on the planet, it was hard to realize why not one had yet been captured.

As he flew over another city on the third day, and saw that it was still debouching refugees, he pondered a possibility. Send a patrol craft down. Intercept a refugee craft, burn the machine, and capture those aboard.

After some thought, he rejected that. In the first place, the Riss machines kept to lanes. That suggested there were "protector" instruments spotted all along the route. No human being could hope to penetrate that line of death. That was also the reason why he refused to consider Czinczar's suggestion that patrols be sent into the enemy camps. The camps also would be protected.

The risk to a few men was quite unimportant, of course. But there was another reason for not testing the danger. He wanted reactions from the Riss. It was they who must force issues against the invader; and by the very nature of the issues they brought up, show what they feared.

On the third day, accordingly, his advice to Czinczar was still, "Wait and follow the pattern."

The passing of that night brought no unexpected developments. By mid-morning, Clane was observing that the refugee traffic had diminished to a trickle of trucking craft. He could imagine the tremendous relief that must be sweeping the populace. They probably believed that they had won the first phase of the engagement, or else regarded the assailant as too foolish to appreciate the advantage he had had.

Let them think what they pleased. Having achieved the safety of wide dispersement, they must now be ready for an active second phase. He was not mistaken in his analysis. Shortly before dark that afternoon, Czinczar sent the long awaited word, "Prisoner captured. When will you be down?"

"Tomorrow," Clane replied.

He spent the rest of the day, and part of the night considering the potentialities. His plans were ready about midnight. At that time he addressed a hundred group captains. It was a very sharp, determined speech. When he had finished, the men were pale, but they cheered him lustily. Toward the end of the question period, one of them asked, "Your excellency, are we to understand that you are planning to be on the ground tomorrow?"

Clane hesitated, then nodded.

The man said earnestly, "I'm sure I speak for my colleagues when I say to you: reconsider. We have talked all this out among us many times during these long months, and it is our opinion that the life of everyone aboard this ship depends upon your excellency remaining alive. No great expedition has ever before been so completely dependent on the knowledge or leadership of one man."

Clane bowed. "Thank you. I shall try to merit the trust reposed in me." He shook his head. "As for your suggestion, I must reject it. I feel that it is necessary for me to question the prisoner we have captured. Why? Because on Earth I dissected the body of one of these beings, and I am probably the only person who knows enough about him for the interview to have any meaning."

"Sir," said the man, "what about Czinczar? We've heard reports of his astuteness."

Clane smiled grimly. "I'm afraid Czinczar will also have to be present at the interview." He broke off. "I'm sorry gentlemen, this argument must cease. For once, the commander must take as great a risk as any of his soldiers. I thought that was one of the dreams of lower ranks."

That brought another cheer, and the meeting broke up a few minutes later with everyone in good humor.

"I don't like this," said Czinczar.

Actually, Clane didn't either. He sat down in a chair, and surveyed the prisoner. "Let's think this over for a while," he said slowly.

The Riss stood proudly—at least that was the impression he gave—in front of his human captors. Clane watched him unhurriedly, preternaturally aware of a number of possibilities. The Riss was about twelve feet from him. He towered like a giant above the powerful barbarian soldiers, and theoretically he could leap forward and tear any individual limb from limb before himself succumbing to an attack.

It was not a point that need be taken too seriously, but still there was such a thing as being prepared for any eventuality. Surreptitiously, he moved his rod of energy into a handier position for defense.

Czinczar said, "It was a little too obvious. The men, of

129

course, were jubilant at catching him, but naturally I asked detailed questions. There's no doubt in my mind that he sought captivity."

Clane accepted the analysis. It was an example of the alertness he expected from the brilliant barbarian leader. And besides, it was the eventuality that had made him take so many precautions.

Theoretically, everything he had done might prove unnecessary. Conversely, if his anxiety was justified, then the precautions would merely provide a first line of defense. In war, the best plans were subject to unbearable friction.

Clane took out his notebook and began to draw. He was not an artist, but presently he handed the rough sketch to a member of his staff who was. The man examined the picture, and then secured a small drawing board from the patrol craft, and began to sketch with quick, sure strokes. When the drawing was finished, Clane motioned the artist to hand it to the Riss.

That huge monstrosity accepted the paper, board and all. He studied it with evidence of excitement, then vibrated the folds of his skin. Watching him, Clane could not decide whether he was showing approval or disapproval.

The Riss continued to study the paper, and finally reached into a fold of his skin and from some hidden receptacle drew out a large pencil. He turned the sheet the artist had used, and drew something on the blank side of the paper. When the Riss had it ready, it was Czinczar who stepped forward and took the drawing from him.

It was not, apparently, his intention to examine it, for he carried it over to Clane without glancing at what was on the paper. As he handed it to the mutation, he bent down for a moment, his back to the Riss, and whispered, "Your excellency, do you realize that the two leaders of this expedition are concentrated here on this spot?"

Clane nodded.

XX

OUT OF THE corner of one eye, Clane caught a brilliant flash of light high in the sky. He glanced quickly around to see if anyone else had noticed it. One of the barbarian officers was craning his neck, but there was an uncertain expression in his face. He had the look of a man who couldn't be sure that what he had seen meant anything.

Clane, who had sat down so that he could, among other things, gaze upward without being too obvious about it, settled slowly back in the chair. He waited tensely for the next flash. It came abruptly. It was almost straight above, which worried him a little. But still he showed no sign.

This time, no one seemed to have observed the flash.

Clane hesitated, and then finally answered Czinczar's question with a question of his own. "Just what," he asked, "do you expect?"

The barbarian leader must have sensed the undertone of excitement in his voice. He looked sharply at Clane. He said slowly, "A Riss has allowed himself to be taken captive. He must have a purpose. That purpose could well be to insure that the forces behind him make their attack at a specific time and place. Why not at the moment and the area where the top leaders of the enemy expedition are interviewing their alien prisoner?"

Clane said, "You feel then that he would be capable of evaluating your rank and mine?" He spoke deliberately. There had been a third flash in the upper sky.

"He can put two and two together," said Czinczar. The barbarian was angry now. He seemed to be aware that he was only partly understanding what was going on. "And remember what Marden said about communicating with the Riss. That suggests they can read our minds. Besides"—he was suddenly sarcastic—"for the first time in our association, you've come like a potentate. You're the one person here sitting down. That's unusual for you on a public occasion. And for the only time in your life that I know about, you've put on the dress clothes of a Linnan temple priest. What are you trying to do—make him realize who you are?"

"Yes," said Clane.

He spoke softly, and then he laughed out loud, exuberantly. "Czinczar," he said at last, more soberly, "this is a test of something I saw during the attack against the Riss battleship on Outland."

"What did you see?" said Czinczar.

"Our molecular weapon showed up as being far more powerful than I had imagined. It did not actually help to destroy the other ship—I used it merely to distract their attention. But it burned away more than a foot of the hard outer shell of the ship wherever it touched. I subsequently discovered that it had a range of some twenty miles, and that aboard the ship it was synchronized to automatic aiming devices."

He showed his even white teeth, as he smiled grimly. "Czinczar," he said, "this entire area is protected by molecular weapons that will with absolute precision burn an atomic bomb out of the sky at a distance of nearly twenty miles."

The barbarian leader's strong face was dark with puzzlement. "You mean, it will explode them that far away?"

"No. It burns them. There is no nuclear explosion, but only a molecular transformation into gas. Being small, the bomb is completely dissipated, the gas is caught by crosscurrents of air and its radioactivity spread over hundreds of square miles."

He expected a strong reaction. He was not mistaken. "Lord Clane," Czinczar said with suppressed excitement, "this is tremendous. All these months we have had this remarkable defensive machine, and didn't know it."

He stopped. Then more slowly, he said, "I'm not going to assume, as I did with the chlorodel, that this is the answer to our requirements. A big ship like our own could fly over a solid rank of such weapons. It might suffer serious but not crippling damage, and it could come low enough for its protective space-time resonators to exterminate everyone below. What is our defense against that? Burrowing?"

"As fast as we can," said Clane, "we dive into the individual caves that your men have been digging, and crouch under several yards of rock."

Czinczar was frowning again. "All this doesn't explain the why of this byplay with our prisoner. Are you trying to force them to an attack?"

Clane savored the opportunity briefly, then he said quietly, "The attack has been on for nearly five minutes."

Having spoken, he raised the drawing the Riss had made and pretended to study it.

Around him, the wave of excitement reached its peak. Men called to each other shrilly. The echoes of the sounds receded into the distance, as other men farther away took up the cry.

During the entire period of turmoil, Clane appeared to be examining the drawings. Actually, with a singleness of purpose he watched the Riss captive.

The guards had forgotten the huge alien. They stood, craning their necks, staring up into the sky, where the flashes had become more numerous. With one word, Clane could have recalled them to their duty. But he decided against saying anything.

The question was, how would the creature react when he finally realized that the atomic attack was a complete fizzle?

For a few seconds, the monster maintained his calm, proud bearing. Then he tilted his head back, and stared earnestly up. That lasted less than half a minute. Abruptly, his gaze came down from the upper air, and he looked quickly around him. For a moment his swift eyes focused on Clane, who blinked rapidly, but did not look away.

It was an effective device. His bent head suggested that he was immersed in the drawing. By blinking his eyelids, he partially concealed the fact that his eyeballs were rolled up high into their sockets. The Riss' gaze passed over him, and the Riss made his first purposeful move.

He reached into a fold of his skin, started to draw something out—and stopped, as Clane said softly almost under his breath, "Don't do it. Stay alive! I know you came here to

133

sacrifice yourself, but it's not necessary now. It would serve no useful purpose. Stay alive and listen to what I have to say."

He didn't expect too much from that. Telepathic communications between an alien who could read minds and a human being who couldn't must surely be a fragile thing. Nevertheless, though he still did not look directly at the Riss, he saw that the creature continued to hesitate.

More firmly, but still under his breath, Clane said, "Remember the drawing. I still don't know what your reaction was—I can't take the time to look—but I suspect it was negative. Think that over. A first judgment isn't necessarily best. Five thousand years ago, man and Riss nearly destroyed each other. And now, the Riss have taken actions that will start the whole struggle over again. So far we have not dropped a single bomb, nor have we used the resonator. That was deliberate. That was designed to show that this time human beings want a different arrangement. Tell your people that we come as friends."

And still it was hard to tell what the reaction was. The alien remained as he had been, one "hand" hidden in the folds of his skin. Clane did not underestimate the possibilities. In dissecting the body of the dead Riss on Earth, he had discovered natural skin pockets big enough to conceal energy rods.

He had warned Czinczar to be on guard, but had asked him not to make a search. The important thing was that the Riss feel free to act.

Beside him, Czinczar said in a monotone, "Your excellency, I think our captive is nerving himself to do something violent. I've been watching him."

So at least one other person had not forgotten the danger. Before Clane could speak, Czinczar went on, sharply, "Your excellency, I urge you to take no chances. Kill him before he pulls a surprise on us."

"No," said Clane. His voice was on a conversational level. "I intend to give him a patrol craft, if he'll accept it, and let him escape. The choice is up to him."

As he spoke, he raised his head for the first time, and gazed squarely at the Riss. The creature's huge, glittering eyes glared back at him. There seemed little doubt but that he knew what was expected of him.

The conflict between his will to live and the unconscious attitudes and beliefs that had brought him here to sacrifice himself was terrible to see. He grew visibly rigid in every muscle.

There was no immediate change in the tense tableau. The Riss stood on a rock ledge looking up at Clane and Czinczar who were higher up on that barren and uneven hillside. Beyond the alien, the tents of the barbarian soldiers were partly visible among the rocks. They stretched as far as the eye could see. A minute went by. The very passage of time, it seemed finally to Clane, was favorable. He relaxed ever so slightly, and said to Czinczar, "I'd like to know what he drew in answer to the drawings I had made up. Will you look at them, while I watch him? I imagine you'll have to study mine first if you hope to understand his reply."

Though he had not said so, he was also interested in the barbarian's own reaction.

Without taking his gaze from the Riss, he held up the drawing board. Czinczar took it, and said presently, "I'm looking at your drawing. There are three planets shown here. One is completely shaded. One is all white, and on the third the mountain areas are shaded, and the foothills and flat sections are white. Am I right in thinking these drawings *are* meant to represent planets?"

"Yes," said Clane.

He waited. After a little, Czinczar said, "The legend at the bottom of the sheet shows the figure of a human being, and opposite that a white rectangle, and below that a Riss with a shaded rectangle opposite his figure."

"That's the explanatory legend," said Clane.

There was a long pause, longer than Clane expected from a man so astute. And yet, on second thought, he was not surprised. It was a matter of attitudes and beliefs. It was the whole nerve process of accepting a radically new notion. The reaction that came finally did not surprise him in the slightest.

"But this is ridiculous," Czinczar said angrily. "Are you seriously suggesting that Riss and human beings share one out of every three planets?"

"That's just a guess," said Clane. He made no further attempt to justify the idea. Fifty centuries before, Riss and human had not even been prepared to share a galaxy. The mental attitude involved seemed to be one of the few things that had survived a holocaust war.

He waited. When the barbarian spoke again, there was satisfaction in his voice. "Your excellency, I am examining his answer. He has drawn three planets, all shaded in. I'd say he rejects your suggestion of sharing."

Clane said steadily, "He's had time to transmit my plan by mental telepathy. The idea may spread rather rapidly. That's all I can hope for at the moment."

Actually, the basic situation was quite different from what it had been long ago. This time, men and Riss alike could look back and see the disaster that had befallen their ancestors.

This time, one man believed in co-operation.

One man, sitting here on this distant enemy planet, accepted the reality that there would be difficulties. Accepted the rigid intolerance of man and Riss alike. Knew that he would be regarded as a fool, enemy of his kind. And still he had no intention of yielding his idea.

He saw himself poised for one minute of eternity at the very apex of power. In all man's history, this moment, this combination of events, had never occurred before, and possibly never would again. A few years from now what he knew of science would be common knowledge, shared by thousands of technicians. It would have to be, if the human race hoped to survive in competition or co-operation with the Riss. Already, he had trained scores of officers. The trouble was, because of his greater background, he learned a dozen things while they learned one.

That fact shaped the difference. Therein lay the tremendous opportunity. Culturally, industrially, that was bad for the human race. Politically, it made the moment.

No one could stop him. None could deny him. He was Lord Clane Linn, potential Lord Leader, commander in chief of the *Solar Star*, the only man who understood something about all the machinery aboard. He had never felt more alert, never sharper of mind, and he hadn't been sick for years.

Czinczar cut across his thought, a note of exasperation in his voice. "Your excellency, if all your schemes didn't work out so well, I'd say you were mad. The Riss attack against us here has been tactically and strategically wrong, not well planned, not well conducted. There have been no explosions for several minutes. If I were the commander on the other side, what has already happened would be only the beginning of a major assault. Logically, there is no limit to the sacrifice a race should make in defending its planet."

He went on in a puzzled tone, "There's something about the attack that we're not seeing, a factor which they're taking into account, but we're not. It's holding them back."

He broke off. He said ironically, "But what about this fellow? How can you solve the problem of the Riss galactically if you can't even persuade this one individual?"

Clane said quietly, "All he's got to do to get a patrol ship is bring his hand out into the open, slowly, inoffensively—"

He stopped. Because the "hand" was coming out. The Riss stood for a moment, studying Clane. Then he walked over to the patrol vessel Clane had mentally indicated. Silently, they watched him get into it, and take off.

When he had gone, Czinczar said, "Well, what now?"

The barbarian leader had a habit of asking such disconcerting questions.

XXI

CLANE RETURNED to the *Solar Star*, and considered. What *should* the next move be?

Go home? It seemed too soon.

He spent half an hour playing with baby Braden. The child fascinated him. "Here," he thought, not for the first time, "is the secret of all progress."

At the moment Braden had no ideas of his own, no unchanging attitudes or beliefs—except possibly those that derived from the way the nurses and Madelina had handled him. There were possible subtle responses to rough or gentle treatment that should not be lightly dismissed.

But he knew nothing of his origin. He did not hate the

Riss. Brought up with a young Riss, the two might even develop friendly relationships—though that was not an important solution to the Riss-human problem. It couldn't be carried out on a big enough scale. Besides, it would be limited by other associations.

He left the baby finally, and settled down in a chair in the control room. There, surrounded by the panoply of instruments that controlled great machines, he told himself, "It's a matter of integrating what I know."

He had a feeling about that. It seemed to him that virtually all the facts were now available. There was one possible exception. What Czinczar had said about the unsatisfactory extent of the Riss attack.

Frowning, he went over in his mind the sequence of events on this Riss planet. And Czinczar was right, he decided.

He was still thinking about it when the radio clerk brought him a message.

Dear Lord Clane:
    More prisoners have been captured. I urge you to come down immediately. I have the missing factor.

                                                        Czinczar.

Clane made his landing shortly after lunch. Barbarian guards herded the prisoners from a small pocket in the rocky hillside.

They sidled over, skinny, bright-eyed men with a feverish look about them. They were unmistakably human. Czinczar made the introduction. His golden voice held the full flavor of the occasion.

"Your excellency, I want you to meet the descendants of the human beings who used to occupy this planet—before it was captured by the Riss five thousand years ago."

Clane had had just a moment's warning—that one look at the prisoners as they came up. It was all he needed. His mind took the impact of the introduction. He was able after a moment to study them, and it seemed to him that he had never seen such wretched-looking human beings. The tallest of the group—there were eight of them—was no more than five feet three. The shortest was a little old wizened individual about four feet six. It was he who spoke.

"Hear you come from Eart'."

138

His accent was so different from the Linnan, that his words sounded like gibberish. Clane glanced at Czinczar, who shrugged, smiled, and said, "Say, yes."

Oddly, the meaning came through then, and thereafter a painfully slow conversation was possible.

"You're the big boy?" the creature said.

Clane thought that over, and nodded. The little old man came closer, pursed his lips, and said hoarsely, "I'm the big boy of *this* bunch."

He must have spoken too loudly. One of the other men, who had been standing by, stirred, and said, in an outraged tone, "Yeah? Listen, Glooker, you do the talkin', we do the fightin'. If there's any big boy in this bunch, it's me."

Glooker ignored the interruption, and said to Clane, "Nothin' but intrigue and complaint all the time. By the holy sphere, you can't do a thing with them."

Clane's mind jumped back to the desperate political and economic intrigue of Linn. He started to say with a smile, "I'm afraid intrigue is a common heritage of limited associative balance—" he stopped. He did a mental double-take, caught himself, and said with a tense calmness, "By the *what?*"

"The sphere. You know, it rolls up and down. It's the one thing that never changes."

Clane had complete surface control of himself again. He said, "I see. You must show it to us sometime."

He turned casually to Czinczar, "Did you know about this?"

Czinczar shook his head. "I talked to them for an hour after they were brought in, but they never mentioned it."

Clane hesitated, then drew the barbarian aside. "Brief me," he said.

The picture was ordinary enough. Man had gone underground. During the long struggle, gigantic machines had created a universe of caves. Long after the burrowing machines were meaningless hulks of metal, the caves remained.

"But," said Clane, puzzled, "how did they hold off the Riss? Just going into a cave wouldn't be enough."

Czinczar was smiling. "Your excellency," he said, "we proved the method right here on this soil." He waved at the rocky, uneven terrain, the desolation that reached to every

139

horizon. "They had, among other things, the 'protector' device—"

Clane flashed, "You mean, they know how to make them?" He thought of his own fruitless efforts to duplicate the Riss alloys.

"It's a part of life to them," said Czinczar. "They make the right alloys as a matter of simple training. They fashion them together because . . . well . . . that's the way things are. They *know*."

Clane had a limp feeling of excitement. It was the same story over again. In Linn, spaceships existed in a bow and arrow culture. On Outland, an inconceivably advanced system of transportation, and telepathy, were accepted realities in a simple, agricultural civilization. And now here was the same evidence of scientific wonders as part of a commonplace life. A technique, if remembered and passed on from one generation to the next, was not something marvelous. It was *the* way of doing something.

Such folkways had their limitations, of course. The people did not have open minds. They resisted change. The Outlanders were extreme examples of that. The Linnans as a nation were almost equally set in their decadence. These little people were harder to judge. In their confirmed and desperate existence, they had little opportunity for growth. And so, because of their environment, they were as rigid as any Outlander.

The deeper meanings of such things remained as obscure as ever.

Clane broke his thought. "Let us make arrangements to visit these people in their home, tomorrow."

They flew over country that was rocky and barren at first. Abruptly, the soil grew greener. A river burst into view, and wound along among trees and heavy undergrowth. And still there was no sign of Riss habitation.

Clane commented on it to Glooker. The little man nodded. "Air's too heavy for 'em. But they won't let us have it." He spoke sourly.

The mutation nodded, but said nothing more.

The entrance to the cave surprised him. It was a huge concrete piling constructed against a hillside, plainly visible for miles. Their patrol craft came down outside the range of the resonators, and the erstwhile prisoners went forward alone into the "protected" area. They came back, "photographed" the visitors, and soon they were being led down a brightly lighted concrete causeway. Spindly bodied men and women, pitiful child mites came out of wood and stone cubbyholes to stare with their feverish unhealthy eyes at the procession of strangers.

Clane began to feel his first admiration. The scene was almost literally out of a nightmare. And yet these half humans with their stunted bodies and their desperate, tense, anxious minds, had fought off the science and military might of the Riss empire. They had burrowed into the soil; by withdrawing into that artificial underground world, they had virtually cut themselves off from sunlight. But here they were alive, and as active as ants in an anthill.

They squabbled, fought and intrigued. They had their own caste system. They followed old marriage customs. They lived and loved and reproduced in the very shadow of the Riss menace. Their average life expectancy was about thirty-five Earth years, as near as Clane could calculate it.

The procession came to a larger cave, which was occupied by several women and swarms of children, but only one man. Clane watched alertly as the man, a roly-poly individual with thin lips and hard blue eyes ambled forward. Glooker introduced him obsequiously as Huddah, the "Boss Boy."

The mutation had his own way of measuring conceited individuals. So now he made his first attempt to control the sphere, which these little people had somewhere in this tangle of caverns.

The problem was, was the sphere close enough?

An instant after he had thought the cue, it flashed up over his head. A hundred throats screeched with wonder and awe.

There was no trouble.

On the return trip, Clane ordered Czinczar to re-embark the barbarian army.

"The existence of a remnant human race on this planet," he explained, "points up emphatically what we discovered. Given certain weapons, man can survive a Riss attack. We'll take along enough 'little men' technicians to start construction on Earth of the two main weapons. As more and more people learn the process, we can count on our defenses holding."

141

He added, "That, of course, doesn't give us back our planets. It's unfortunate but the defense weapons will work equally well for the Riss."

He glanced sharply at Czinczar, expecting a reaction. But that barbarian's lean face was impassive. Clane hesitated, then went on, "It is my plan before we leave here to turn out millions of photostats of my drawing, showing how we propose to solve the Riss-human hostility. We'll flutter them down over various cities and over the mountain sides, so that every Riss becomes aware of the basic idea of sharing."

Czinczar made a sound as if he were choking. Clane said quickly, "We mustn't forget the Riss also have a problem. Apparently, they need a more rarefied atmosphere than man. They can stand the dense air at sea level on Earth, and here, but for everyday living they've got to be high up. That greatly limits the habitable areas available to them. Man has not been overly sympathetic to the difficulties involved, in fact aggravated them."

Czinczar broke into speech at last, "How do you mean?"

Clane said slowly, "From all accounts, men of the golden age discovered how to release the oxygen from the crusts of otherwise barren planets and moons. Presumably, the Riss knew how to do that also, but they had a terrible disadvantage. They would want the process to stop sooner than would man. I can just imagine the glee of human beings as they forced an ever thicker atmosphere on planet after planet."

Czinczar said in a remorseless tone, "It is natural that each race fight to the limit for survival."

Clane said sharply, "That's all very well for intelligent beings who think on the animal level. Man and Riss *must* rise above it." He broke off grimly. "You understand, that we will not allow the Riss in the solar system, nor should human beings aspire to share the main Riss system. The home planets have to be inviolate."

"How are we going to get them off?" said Czinczar.

Clane made no direct answer.

Back on the ship, Czinczar offered only one important objection when Clane told him they would have to make a stopover on Outland.

"What about the people of the solar system?" he asked uneasily. "For all we know, a major attack has already taken place. We do know that as of now, human beings have no resonators or energy beams to protect them."

Clane was grim. "It takes time to conquer an inhabited planet. That's what I'm counting on." He added harshly, "If we go back right now, we could only fight the Riss on equal terms. That would be bad for us, since they have the ships and the weapons, and the endless equipment for making more."

"And how will the situation be changed if we go to Outland first?"

"I'm not sure." Clane spoke frankly.

"I see. Another idea at the back of your mind?"

"Yes."

Czinczar was silent for several seconds. Then his eyes showed laughter. "I support it," he said, "sight unseen."

He held out his hand. "Your excellency," he said earnestly, "I'm your man. From this moment on, no more schemes, no opposition. I salute the future Lord Leader of Linn, of whom I herewith request the rank of loyal ally."

It was an unexpectedly complete surrender. Clane blinked, and swallowed hard. Momentarily, he felt overwhelmed. Then he caught hold of himself and said with a faint smile, "I'm not Lord Leader yet. It will take time to make influential people aware of me again. There will probably be a difficult preliminary."

There was no need to elaborate on that. The politically wise barbarian nodded, his lips pursed.

Clane went on, "We now have two spheres, one in reserve on Earth—" His eyes met Czinczar's, seeking confirmation.

The latter agreed. "Yes, two. You can have the one in the solar system at any time."

Clane continued in a firm voice, "As I see it, the sphere is the primitive version of the transport system developed on Outland and Inland."

"And so—"

"Control of the cosmos." Something of the fire of the thought that was in his mind enriched his voice. "Czinczar, have you ever wondered how the Universe functions?"

The barbarian was sardonic. "I was born, I am alive. I shall die. That's my function. Can you alter the pattern?"

Clane smiled wryly. "You strike too deeply, my friend. I'm

just now becoming vaguely aware of the forces that are operating inside me. They're more intricate than the physical sciences. I intend to leave them alone till I have more time."

He paused, frowning. "Perhaps that's an error. How dare a man who doesn't understand himself propose to settle the affairs of the Universe?"

He shrugged. "It can't be helped. My hope right now is that, with the sphere to help him, Marden will be able to teach me their system."

Marden drew back curiously to let the men carrying the sphere and its container enter his house. They set it down, as Clane said, "Ever see anything like this before, Marden?"

Marden was smiling. The sphere rose up from the container, and took up a position over his head. "An artificial opening," he said. "I've heard of them. They were the beginning."

He added, "If I had known you had such a thing as this, I would have taught him"—he nodded at Clane—"how all this works when he first talked about it."

Clane said, "Will it help me to read minds?"

Marden was tolerant. "That will take a few years. The rest you can start doing immediately with the sphere to help you."

Afterwards, Czinczar said, "But how *do* you expect to use the sphere against the Riss? You told me yourself it would not be decisive."

Clane evaded answering. The idea in his mind was so intricate in its scientific concepts, so vast in scope, that he dare not put it into words.

Besides, there was much to do first.

The trip home was long and tiring but not altogether wasted. Several dozen people aboard had gone insane, and there were any number of tangled minds and eccentric characters. Clane studied them, tried techniques of therapy on them—and again and again went back to baby Braden, the wellspring of his own interest.

It seemed to him that in the child he would find the beginning of the normalness and abnormalness of the adult.

The baby made as many movements with his left hand as with his right. He was not interested in objects held farther away than two feet. But if an article was brought closer than that, he would usually—though not always—reach for it, as often with his left hand as with his right.

Given something that he could grab hold of, he could be lifted into the air, his own strength supporting him. He did this equally with either hand, but each time used only his fingers. His thumb was still a useless appendage.

He showed marked symptoms of fear after a loud noise, a pain stimulus, or when subjected to a sudden sense of falling. Nothing else could alarm him. He was not afraid of animals or objects whether large or small, no matter how close they were brought. And he liked being stroked under his chin.

Other babies aboard, given the same tests, responded similarly.

Many times, Clane pondered his observations. "Suppose," he wondered, "that *all* babies turned out to have the same instinctive reactions as Braden and the ones I've tested. In other words, basically they don't seem to be either right-handed or left-handed. They're not afraid of the dark. Apparently, they learn these things. When? Under what conditions? How does one baby become irresponsible Calaj, another one ruthless, brilliant Czinczar, and a third a field laborer?"

There was one way, he discovered, in which Braden differed from the other babies of his own age group. When a blunt object was drawn across the bottom of his foot, all his toes flexed in one direction. Every other baby under a year old flexed the big toe upward and four downward.

The dividing line seemed to be one year of age. Of the nineteen older children Clane tested, sixteen reacted like Braden. That is, their toes all flexed in the same direction. The other three continued to react like normal babies under a year old. Each one of the three was a recognized problem child.

It was highly suggestive to Clane that Braden at four months of age should have the same responses as much older children. Was here perhaps evidence that his son had inherited the supernormal stability which he suspected in himself?

He was still deeply involved in the whole intricate problem of sanity when the *Solar Star* entered Earth's atmosphere. That was nine hundred and seventy days after its departure.

XXII

BEFORE LANDING, Clane sent out patrols. Their reports were encouraging.

His estate was unharmed, though a large and noisy refugee village had grown up starting about two miles from the house.

According to the accounts brought back by the patrol commanders, some four hundred Riss battleships were in the solar system. They had taken possession of most of the mountain areas on the various planets and moons, and were busily consolidating their positions.

There had been no effective resistance. Army units, when cornered or ordered to fight, were wiped out. Human civilians who were sighted by the enemy, or who had been unlucky enough to be on the scene of a landing, were blasted to a man.

Immediately after their arrival, the invaders had made a mass attack on nearly half a hundred cities. About two million people were caught by the hellish atomic explosions; so the report went. The rest successfully reached their farm havens and were safe.

For more than a year, no bombs had fallen. And even in those first deadly days, not a single lowland city was attacked. The Riss concentrated their colossal bombs on foot-hill cities and on mountain cities located less than thirty-five hundred feet above sea level.

The stupid and the thoughtless among the refugees noted both the commissions and the omissions. And for months they had been trickling back to the undamaged centers. There was need for swift action. And yet—Clane shook his head.

And yet he operated within the limitations imposed by his human as well as enemy environment.

"We'll set up defenses around the estate first," Clane told Czinczar. "It'll take about a week to put up the resonators

146

d the molecular weapons, and start work on the caves.
While that's being done, I'll try to get my spy organization
together."

Everything took time, thought and the most careful prep-
ation.

Liftboats hovered in the night. Shadowy figures stood on the
round. Small craft floated down out of the blackness to-
ards lights arranged in a certain pattern. Such rendezvous
ere old in Clane's experience, and he took them calmly. For
ars he had dealt through agents, listened to accounts of
enes witnessed by other eyes than his own, and he had a
racticed skill in building up the resulting pictures, so that
any times he could see things that the spy had not noticed.

Each meeting with an agent followed the same general
attern. The individual remained in the darkness so far as
her agents, also on the scene, were concerned. There were
aves present to insure that the men and women were fed,
it the meal itself was handed through a narrow slit of a
indow to a pair of hands that reached out of the night. The
eal was eaten by a shadowy human being who stood in a
in lineup of his own kind. It was seldom, however, that in-
viduals spoke to each other.

Each agent reported first to three officers. The report was
erbal and delivered out of the darkness to the officers, who
emselves remained hidden by the darkness. If even one of
e tribunal decided that the story merited further consider-
ion, the spy was passed on to Clane.

The next step was precautionary. The agent was searched,
a man, by a man; if a woman, by a woman. Most of the
ents were old at the game and knew each step, so that they
fered no objections when they entered Clane's private patrol
aft and for the first time during the interview, had to show
eir faces.

Gradually, in this way, as the night passed, the over-all pic-
re of the past two and a half years came through to Clane.

The last agent finally departed, and the faint sound of their
all craft was scarcely more than a whisper in the intense
rkness that settled down after the false dawn. Clane re-
rned to the spaceship and considered what he had learned.
Lilidel and Calaj knew of his return. It showed swift spy

147

work on the part of their supporters. But the information
pleased Clane. They would spread the news of his reappear
ance much faster than he could do.

He was not surprised to learn that Lilidel already regarded
him as a deadlier danger than the Riss. To her, government
was a personal possession. The fact that she herself had n
idea what to do in this national emergency meant nothing
Regardless of consequences, she intended to cling to power.

Since it would take time to re-establish his contacts, Clan
presumed that she would have time to take some action. Wit
all the thoroughness of which he was capable, he set abou
the task of plugging up possible loopholes in his defens
system.

To begin with, he concentrated on the refugee village.

XXIII

THE BUSINESS MANAGER of his estate, a former slave, ha
registered for him under the refugee law. The manager, wl
had in his day been a high Martian government official, r
ported that at the time of registration, more than a year befor
he had noticed nothing unusual in the way his papers h
been handled. The picture he gave of hastily organized cleric
staffs working in confusion was typical of other areas whe
the same law had been introduced—without Lilidel bei
aware of it— and it satisfied Clane up to a point.

Because of the acreage of his estate, he had been assign
three hundred families, totaling one thousand ninety-four p
sons. It was a village full of strange people. When he we
down to look them over on the day after his return to the
tate, it seemed to Clane that he had never seen such a mot]
crowd. On inquiry, he discovered that he had been assign
the inhabitants of a section of a single street. On the surfa
that looked fair and seemed to indicate that his farm v

being handled as objectively as were the others. There was a full quota of human beings, sensible and foolish, short and long, fat and thin, clever and stupid—an ordinary cross-section of any city's population.

Clane decided not to let it go at that. It took only one assassin to kill one or more people. Such a man would need only one opportunity, whether gained by chance, or design. It was too easy to kill, and no man or woman in history had ever recovered from that particular type of catastrophe.

He concentrated the attention of nearly half his spies and slowly, as the days passed and the reports came in, realized that he had given them an assignment which could never be satisfactorily completed.

He had a file made up for each family and in each file he had trained clerks enter the information that came in about individual members of the family. It became apparent that part of each person's life history was not available.

In his determination to penetrate that darkness, he organized a bulletin board newspaper, full of chatty information about the doings and backgrounds of the members of the group. As the new village grew, his spies, taking on the role of friendly reporters, interviewed each adult and each child over ten years old, ostensibly for the bulletin. Some of the spies considered the age limit too low, but Clane was insistent. The history of Linn, particularly of more ancient times, was full of accounts of the bravery of very young people in times of emergency.

His hope was that he might isolate the assassin. He looked for hesitation and reluctance in answering questions. He wanted the diffident refugee marked off as a person who had possibly murderous reasons for withholding information.

As it turned out, the agents listed as suspects seventeen men and nine women. Clane had them arrested and set down in a more distant area.

And still he was not satisfied.

"It isn't," he told Madelina unhappily, "that I'm abandoning the proposition that people must rise above themselves in this crisis. But a few unco-operative individuals could cause disaster."

She patted his arm affectionately. She said, "What a man you are for worrying."

She was a slim, straight girl at this time, with a fine, sensitive face. All her emotional intensity remained, but it was concentrated now in the normal channels of husband and child. She embraced him abruptly, impulsively.

"Poor sweetheart, you have to think of so many things, don't you?"

That day, also, went by without incident. Through his spies, Clane watched every horizon of human activity. The reports from Golumb, where the government was, stifled once and for all any will he might have had to co-operate with the Lilidel group.

The incredible Calaj had brought back the games. Men and animals were once more dying in the arena to provide sport for the court. At night, government buildings were converted into theaters and dance halls. Often, the merrymakers were still at play when the clerks arrived in the morning to begin work. The Lord Adviser had taken an interest in the army. Thousands of men were being drilled, so that they could assume formations which spelled out phrases like "The People Love Calaj."

Over in the mountains, a second Riss expedition arrived. Thousands of monsters disembarked. Czinczar, who reported the arrival, sent along an appeal:

Your Excellency:
How are you going to drive these creatures from the solar system if you do not even have control of Linn?
Please take action without delay.

Clane replied that he was training clerks for the first phase of government seizure. He pointed out that it was an intricate task. "A leader," he wrote, "has to work with human beings. This limits all his actions and controls his destiny. As you must know better than most people, I have tried to transcend such obstacles. I have thought in terms inviting men to do their duty to the race, and disregard such things as who shall be boss and who shall obey. I still hope that we will have such a spontaneous demonstration of will-to-co-operate for the benefit of all such as has not been seen in generations.

"At the moment, in spite of the risks, I am moving forward

a step at a time. I agree with you that it is essential that I have control of the state for some years."

He had barely dispatched the message when one of his guards in a patrol craft made an emergency landing in the garden, and reported that a score of Linnan spaceships were approaching.

Even as he told of them, the dark shapes of the large naval vessels grew visible in the distance.

XXIV

THEY CAME in four lines of five each, and settled on the ground about four and a half miles from the house. They had landed in such a way that their air locks faced away from the estate. For a while there was a great deal of activity that Clane couldn't see. He guessed that men were disembarking.

Just how many men, it was difficult to decide. On space flights, these big machines carried complements of only two hundred officers and soldiers. But on such short trips as this fifteen hundred or two thousand per ship was possible.

It quickly became apparent that a very large number of men indeed was involved, for within an hour hundreds of groups of them swarmed over the hill and began to spread out in an enveloping movement.

Clane watched them uneasily through his Riss vision system. It was one thing to have a defense system that could kill every man now approaching. It was quite another actually to kill them.

The possibility that he might have to do so brought a return of his old anger. He wondered grimly if the human race deserved to be perpetuated. As in the past, he decided in favor; and so there seemed nothing to do but to warn the approaching army.

Both the molecular beams and the resonators were set to

react in their terrific fashion at two miles against all craft to which they were not attuned.

He flew alone to that perimeter, taking a loud-speaker hookup with him. He set the Riss lifeboat to follow a course just within the death line. At a hundred yards, he was not completely out of range of a good archer, but the metal walls of the machine would give ample protection.

The men nearest him were now little more than two hundred yards away. Clane rumbled out his first warning. In a clear, mechanical voice, he described the line of death, indicating trees, shrubs and other landmarks that constituted the perimeter. He urged those within hearing to send warnings to soldiers farther away. He finished that first urgent message with the words:

"Test this. Send animals across, and watch the result."

He didn't wait for their reaction, but flew on to make sure that other groups also received the same warning. When he turned back, he saw that it had stopped them about fifty yards from the demarking line. Consultations took place. Presently, messengers in small, fast ships flew from group to group. Satisfied, Clane settled to the ground, and waited.

There was another pause in the activity of the groups of soldiers, and then a small patrol ship landed among the nearest group. Traggen climbed out of it and stood with a megaphone in his hands. He started forward, but he must have known of the warnings for he stopped after proceeding less than ten yards. He raised the megaphone and shouted, "The Lord Adviser Calaj, who is personally commanding these troops, orders you to surrender immediately."

It was interesting to Clane that as far as the eye could see there was no sign of anyone even remotely resembling the Lord Adviser Calaj. He said, "You tell his excellency, the Lord Adviser Calaj, that his uncle would like to talk to him."

Traggen said coldly, "His excellency does not talk to outlaws."

Clane said quickly, "Have I been declared an outlaw?"

Traggen hesitated. Clane did not wait for him to answer.

He called, "Please inform his excellency, Lord Calaj, that unless he comes forward to talk to me, I shall ride along the perimeter here telling the truth about him to the soldiers."

Clane paused with a wry smile. "I forgot," he said, "you

can't tell him that, can you? Better put it like this. Tell him that I threaten to fly along and tell *lies* about him to the soldiers."

He finished, "I'll give him ten minutes, so you'd better hurry."

Traggen hesitated and then turned and went back to his machine. It rose from the ground, and flew back towards the ridge more than two miles away. Clane did not bother to watch it land. He flew up and down in front of the soldiers, pausing before each group to tell a ribald joke about himself. In analyzing the popularity of certain of his officers, during the barbarian war, he had assumed that no officer could actually be liked for himself alone—the average soldier simply didn't have the opportunity to find out much about the real character of his commander.

So it must be something else. He watched and listened, and finally selected a number of coarse jests which poked fun at authority. Simply by telling one or two of them, he changed the attitude toward him of most of the soldiers who heard his pep talks. According to reports, he came to be regarded as a good fellow. He wasn't, but that made no difference. The so-called humor was a magic key to their good will.

Civilians, naturally, had to be handled differently, a fact which old soldiers sometimes forgot.

The question was, would these men, who had been with Jerrin on the planets, who knew little or nothing of what Lord Clane Linn had done against Czinczar, and who were now supposed to capture him—would they also laugh at his jokes?

They did, almost to a man. Entire groups rocked with laughter. A few officers tried sternly to stop them, but they were outnumbered. At the end of ten minutes, Clane returned to his original stopping point, satisfied that he had done what he could to turn the men in his favor.

Just what good it would do was another matter.

He forgot that, for a long, strange and wonderful procession was approaching.

First of all came scores of brightly colored patrol craft. They gyrated as they flew, like a well organized pyrotechnic display. In a final chromatic swirl, they gracefully took up positions directly in front of Clane. It was skillfully, even brilliantly, done, so that not until they were stationary did he realize their new position spelled out one word. The word was "C A L A J."

And now came the most wonderous machine of all—a large, open-decked patrol ship. It was a flower float, gorgeously done up. A little ornate, perhaps, a little out of key, and rather too magnificent for its purpose—Clane assumed that its purpose was to set off the Lord Adviser.

That was an error in judgment on Calaj's part. He was hardly noticeable. He had selected a bright uniform that blended in rather well with the flowers. The red coat could have been a design of carnations or roses, or any one of a dozen flowers. The blue and yellow striped trousers were well matched by nearly half a score of similarly colored floral decorations.

It seemed clear that the new Lord Adviser had already achieved for himself the dangerous environment where no one dared to advise him.

As Clane watched, the colorful monstrosity of a ship settled to the ground. Other craft landed all around it, and presently Traggen came forward with a megaphone.

"His excellency, Lord Calaj in person, orders you to surrender."

The farce was to continue.

Clane answered, loudly enough for Calaj to hear, "Tell the child in the flower box that I want to talk to him."

As Traggen turned indecisively back to the flower boat, Clane saw Calaj pick up a megaphone. A moment later his shrill voice commanded nearby soldiers to go farward and seize Clane.

"Have no fear," Calaj finished boldly. "His only power is that of hypnosis, and you don't have to worry about that. I've got a cage here for him. Lock him inside it, and bring him back to me."

Clane smiled to himself, grimly. Calaj had apparently explained to himself why he had been so subservient the last time he and his uncle had met. Hypnosis. It was a simple method for covering up weakness.

Clane waited for the reaction to the boy's commands.

Both the soldiers of the group and their officers seemed uncertain. There was no display of dash and *élan*, no eager surge forward to show the commander in chief that here were men ready and willing to die for him. The officers gazed un-happily at Traggen, but if they expected him to help them, they were mistaken. Traggen snatched up his megaphone, and bellowed through it, "You will obey the commands of your Lord Adviser, or suffer the consequences."

That brought action. A dozen soldiers, with one officer in command, ran toward the flower ship and removed the cage from it. A patrol vessel darted forward, and the cage was put aboard. The men climbed over the railing, and the boat darted toward Clane.

As it reached the death perimeter, there was a puff of flame. Where the boat had been, a haze of ashes settled slowly toward the ground.

"Next!" said Clane implacably.

There was a pause and then an angry shout from Calaj. "Hypnosis," he yelled at another group of men. "Pay no atten-tion. Go in there and get him."

The men hung back, but their officers seemed in some curious way to have accepted Calaj's explanation. Savagely, they ordered their men into patrol boats, and being Linnan officers, they climbed in with them. Whatever blindness afflicted them, it had nothing to do with lack of courage.

This time two boats came forward, and were destroyed in that instantaneous fashion.

Clane spoke through his loudspeaker hookup into the si-lence: "Traggen, the atom gods will continue to defend me against all the attacks you can mount. If you want to save your legion, try to convince his excellency that I have no con-trol over this tragedy. I can merely warn you that the gods themselves will protect me against anything that you and he and all the foolish people who raised him to power can do against me. Take heed!"

Calaj must have heard, because he shrilled, "The army will attack in one group. We'll overwhelm this traitor's hypnotic tricks."

To Clane, it was a dismaying command. He had hoped that even the boy would realize the futility of further attack. But apparently that was too much to expect. Now, it was up to him to choose between Calaj and the army. The repercus-sions that would follow if he were actually forced to kill the youth were unpredictable. It might seriously slow down

155

the pattern he had set himself for taking over the government.

At the moment, one possibility remained to be explored.

He settled himself at the weapon control board of the Riss liftboat. The aiming devices spun and pointed as he manipulated them with the deftness of much practice.

A spume of blue flame gashed the grass beside Calaj's gorgeously beflowered craft.

Through his microphone, he called derisively, "Your excellency, does it feel like hypnosis when it's this close?"

The grass was burning. Even from where Clane watched, the soil looked fused.

In the flowery float, Calaj climbed to his feet and lazily walked up to the side of his craft, and looked down at the flames. Then he raised his megaphone.

"You just have to look at them," he said, "and they disappear." His voice went up: "Attack the traitor!"

It was a rather magnificent bluff. Somehow, out of the depths of confusion that was in him, the boy had dredged the outer appearance of confidence that no leader could be without if he hoped to operate with a field army.

Carefully, Clane aimed. The side of the craft opposite Calaj flared with a ravenous fire. The heat must have been terrific, for the two pilots tumbled out of their seats, and dived over the front of the boat. Their clothes were smoking.

Calaj cringed, but did not immediately budge. Clane was shaken. His hope of an easy solution was fading; and the Lord Adviser's bravery was having its effect. If Calaj were killed now, he could well be regarded as having died a hero's death.

Clane hesitated. The next step had to be the decisive one. If he aimed even a few feet too close, Calaj would either die or be desperately injured.

Clane spoke into his microphone, "Calaj," he said, "I suggest that you suddenly decide it isn't hypnosis, and say that further action must await study of the situation."

The suggestion was fortunately timed. The fire was spreading. Most of the flowers at the front and side were burning, and the flames had caught firmly on what must be a wooden deck. A gust of smoke engulfed Calaj, and there was evidently heat in it, for he retreated a few feet, and began to cough just like any person breathing smoke instead of air.

He made the mistake, then, of putting a handkerchief over his mouth. And that seemed to convince him that his bluff could not be carried on.

With surprising dignity, he lowered himself over the side of the boat, walked clear of the fire—and arrogantly motioned Traggen to come to him.

There was a brief consultation, after which Calaj climbed into one of the colorful patrol boats that had accompanied him. The machine took off, and headed towards the distant line of spaceships. Traggen called over the commanders of the nearest groups of soldiers, and there were more consultations, after which the officers rejoined their units.

The army began to withdraw. In about an hour and a half there was not a man in sight. Just before dusk the first spaceship took off. One by one the others followed. In the gathering darkness, it was hard to decide just when the last ship departed. But one thing seemed clear. The battle was over.

He had thought the problem of Lilidel and Calaj was over also. But when he reached the house he found disaster. A stretcher had just been carried up to the patio.

On it lay the corpse of Madelina.

XXV

IN DEATH, she looked like a young girl asleep, her hair slightly disheveled, her body slack, her arms limply cradling her head.

Clane looked down at her, and felt something of his own life go out of him. But his voice was steady as he asked, "How did it happen?"

"In the refugee village, half an hour ago."

Clane frowned over that, and it was several seconds before

the reason for his puzzlement struck him. He said then, "But what was she doing down there?"

"A message came up inviting her to come and see a new baby."

"Oh!" said Clane. And though the other's voice went on, he heard nothing more for a time.

He was thinking drearily: *Of course, that would be the method.*

The Mother Madelina, the chatelaine of the estate, the lady bountiful—into all these roles Madelina had channeled her intense emotional nature. And the astute Lilidel, gazing from afar through the eyes and ears of her spies, had realized the potentialities. A frontal attack to distract *his* attention, and if that didn't work, at least she would have struck one deadly blow. Or perhaps the attack on him had been Calaj's idea, and Lilidel had merely utilized the opportunity.

He grew aware again of the voice of the guards' captain making his report. "Your excellency," the officer was saying, "she insisted on going. We took all possible precautions. Guards went into the house, and found the woman, her husband and the baby. When the Lady Madelina entered the bedroom, the mother of the baby said, 'Do we have to have all these soldiers in here?' Immediately, the Lady Madelina pushed the guards into the outer room, and closed the door. She must have been stabbed the moment the door was closed, for she uttered no cry. She died without knowing it."

"And the assassin?" Clane asked drably.

"We became suspicious in less than a minute. Some of our soldiers broke open the door. Others ran outside. The murderers were very skillful. The husband had gone to the back of the house where there was a patrol boat. The woman must have climbed out of the window. They were out of sight before we could commandeer another boat, or reach any of our own ships. The pursuit is already on, but I shall be surprised if it is successful."

Clane doubted it, too. "Have they been identified yet?"

"Not yet. But they must have been refugees, planted in the village for just such a purpose."

He had the grave dug on the hill where Joquin, his long-dead tutor, was buried. On the headstone was engraved the epitaph:

After the burial, he sat for a timeless period on the grass beside the grave, and for the first time considered his own responsibility in the assassination. He could have taken more precautions.

He abandoned that line quickly, for it was fruitless. One man could do only so much.

His final conclusion was simple. He was back in Linn, with all the deadly intrigue that implied. In spite of all his skill, Lilidel and Calaj had successfully worked an old trick on him. They had done so on the eve of his attempt to take over the government.

There seemed nothing to do but carry through with the plan.

Lord Clane Linn set up his headquarters in a village. The village was located a mile from the outskirts of Golomb, the town where the government had taken refuge.

He established his office in a large one-story house that sprawled comfortably back from a little dirt road. There were tall trees around the house, and in their shelter many tents were swiftly erected. A huge barn at the back of the house was big enough to hold numerous small aircraft.

On the other side of the dirt road was a many-storied inn with a capacity of more than a hundred people, and dining room space to feed hundreds.

Clane set up a night and day patrol of Riss liftboats. With their terrific fire power they dominated all approaches to the village.

Guards patrolled the fields and roads. Clerks in great numbers began to arrive the first day, and each day there were more of them. Mostly, they were from his own estate, but some were hired locally. By the second day, he had organized a pool of a hundred messenger craft, and he was ready to start work.

From the beginning he made literally no mistakes intellectually. His tremendous experience stood him in good stead. On the level of action, he did the right thing almost automatically, almost without thinking.

Physically, it was a different story. He was tired all the time.

He ignored the symptoms. He forced himself to prolonged effort.

And on that second day he wrote one letter, and dispatched a hundred copies of it over the planet to men who had been his leading supporters. His words were friendly but firm. He suggested that all those in authoritative positions submit copies to him of any reports they made to the government, and that they pass on to him all official orders or documents which they, in turn, received.

His letter contained no direct suggestion that he was usurping the function of the government, but the implication must have been plain. Within a few hours answering messages began to arrive from the nearest provinces. Nearly three quarters of the replies were statements of unconditional allegiance. The rest took the same attitude but more cautiously.

Before night of that second day several score great men came personally to congratulate him on his action, and to swear that they would support him to the death.

Hour by hour the excitement and tension mounted. Clane retired late, and though he fell asleep almost immediately, he dreamed strange, terrifying dreams of his childhood. All through that long night, he tossed and turned restlessly. And in the morning he wakened with the feeling that he had not slept at all.

He emerged from his bedroom, feeling worn out even as the long day began.

He found that messages had poured in continuously throughout the hours of darkness. These were from the more remote districts. From the number of them, it seemed to Clane that each person to whom he had written must have advised dozens of other supporters in his territory.

By mid-morning the avalanche of messages made it necessary to take over part of the inn, and hurriedly to fly more clerks from his estate.

Clane ate lunch with a sense of victory. From where he sat at the window of the inn restaurant, he could see men coming and going, and converted pleasure and military craft flying low over the trees. It seemed as if every minute a machine was landing or leaving.

Here and there makeshift buildings were being hastily put up, as able administrators took all the necessary steps to fit themselves into the pattern of his actions.

Shortly after lunch, Clane sent out his second letter, this time to governors, government officials and important personages who had not previously supported him. It was differently worded than the first. Coolly, curtly, he advised the recipients of the location of his headquarters. He ended his note with the directive:

Please be advised that duplicates of all documents which you submit to Calaj must in future be sent to me. You will also forward any messages or documents which you receive from the Calaj government, after first taking a copy for your own files.

The implications of that letter would not be lost on astute individuals. Hundreds of cautious men would size up the situation and act according to their private interests and beliefs.

The response was astounding. Within two hours not only messages but the men themselves began to arrive. Patrons, governors, military commanders, staff officers, government officials—all the rest of that day and throughout the evening, Clane's small headquarters was jammed with men eager to switch their allegiance now that they were certain there was someone to whom they could switch it.

Clane went to bed that night, more exhausted than he had been at any time since Madelina's death. But the question, the doubt, that had been in his mind for so many years, was answered, was resolved.

He had struck the spark, touched the vital chord. And men had responded—as he had hoped they would.

It was time. Oh, but it was time. It was a quarter of twelve for the race of man.

But they *had* responded. He slept tensely. And woke wondering if he would have the strength to do the ten thousand things that still had to be done. In a few, brief years all these human beings must learn to accept their great role in the stellar universe.

The parade of new supporters through his office resumed shortly after dawn. As the overcrowded conditions increased, a famous Patron suggested that Clane transfer his headquarters to Golomb into a government building of more suitable size. "It will be easier that way," he urged. "There, liaison has already been established between the various departments."

Clane agreed, and announced that he would make his move the following day.

By mid-afternoon, some of the strain was off him. Ranking officials set up offices for the sole purpose of receiving new men and assigning them to their duties. It was a task which Clane had handled almost singlehanded until then.

He began to receive reports of Lilidel's bewilderment at the way government men were disappearing from the official residence. Just when she had her first inkling of the truth, Clane did not discover. But he was not too surprised when she turned up in person on the fifth morning, less than an hour before he was due to make his move to Golomb.

The man who announced her said cynically, within her hearing, "Your excellency, a woman who claims to be your sister-in-law wants to see you."

It was a cruel remark, particularly since the man who uttered it had transferred his allegiance only the day before.

"Send her in," was all Clane said.

The woman who staggered into his office was but vaguely recognizable as Lilidel. Her face was blotched. Her eyes were wide open, too wide; and the skin around them was discolored as if she had spent a sleepless night. She was furious and terrified by turns.

"You mad man!" she shrieked. "How dare you try to take over the legal government."

The phrase obsessed her. She and Calaj *were* the "legal government". It was all she could think of, and it was not until she was persuaded to sit down that she grew calm enough for Clane to disillusion her. She listened to his words with the visible fright of a person who was being sentenced to death.

Gently, Clane explained that in a crisis governments fell

162

because they could not help themselves. "Sometimes," he went on, "when a weak ruler does not interfere too much with the power of efficient subordinates, his government can survive a minor storm, but in time of national danger an inadequate government tumbles like a house of cards."

Towards the end of his explanation, she must have stopped listening, for she began to shout again, about what she was going to do to the traitors.

"I've ordered Traggen to execute them all," she said in a voice that trembled with the violence of her fury.

Clane shook his head, and said quietly, "I also sent an order to Traggen this morning. I ordered him to bring Calaj here to me, alive, today. Let us see whose command he will obey."

Lilidel stared at him for a moment. Then she shook her head wonderingly and mumbled, "But we're the *legal* government."

Her next action indicated what she thought Traggen's choice would be. Her eyes closed. Her head sagged. Slowly, she crumpled to the floor at Clane's feet.

Calaj, when he was brought in late in the afternoon, was insolent. He sat down in a chair. He leaned back. He said, "Do the gods still love me, uncle?"

Clane was fascinated. He had watched such one-sided growth as this before. It showed how human beings responded to a new environment. For nearly three years, Calaj had been nominally Lord Adviser. With the possible exception of Lilidel, the people who had put him in power had all planned to use a naïve youth for their own purposes. How desperately they had been mistaken.

Clane wasted no time on the young monster. He had already sent Lilidel to a rest home that he maintained in a remote province. Now, under escort, he sent Calaj to join her.

There seemed no limits to the work that had to be done. The reports that came in, even when abbreviated for him, took time to read and time to understand. Gradually, however, even as he grew progressively more weary, the overall picture emerged.

From all that he could gather, the first phase of the Riss invasion was over. The arrival of a second horde of colonists, he was convinced, emphasized that the second phase was due to begin. It would be remorseless. It would be aimed at every large community. Ships with resonators need only fly low over the land, and men would die by the millions.

Therefore—attack the Riss.

But he had caught a chest cold, which he seemed unable to throw off. Feeling sicker than he cared to admit, Clane headed for his estate. He settled down for what he intended to be a brief rest.

It seemed the worst thing he could have done. He coughed steadily, and almost choked with phlegm. His head ached until he could hardly think. At times his vision grew so blurred he could see only with the greatest difficulty.

It became impossible for him to retain solid foods. He was forced on a diet of liquids only. On the evening of the second day, sicker than he had ever been before in his life he went to bed.

He was still convinced that all he needed was rest.

This, Clane told himself shakily, *is ridiculous.*

It was morning of his third day abed. Through the open window he could hear the sounds of men working in the garden. Twice, during a period of minutes, a woman's musical laughter floated in on the still, sweet air.

His eyes ached, his body felt feverish and chilled by turns. He was miserable to the point of not caring what happened to him. He had the vague feeling that he had made a mistake in coming back to the estate; the *Solar Star* would have been a better haven. Better equipped, more trained chemists. Something might have been done for him.

The idea never came into sharp focus. It was just something he should have done. All he could do now was sweat it out.

He had a passing thought: *The trouble is, I've never been sick before. I've no experience. I didn't realize that disease weakens the mind.*

He stirred wearily, lying there in the bed. *I've got to get well,* he urged himself, *I'm the only one who can drive the Riss from Earth. If I should die—* But he dared not think of that.

Wryly, he pictured himself, the despised mutation risen

164

to the greatest office in the empire of Linn. And in the hour of victory against a deadly enemy struck down into his bed. Here he was, held helpless by a weakness within his own body greater than any power that he could ever wield outside.

And the victory was fading, slipping, evaporating, with him.

Shaking his head, very dispirited, he turned on his side and went to sleep.

He dreamed that he was a child of four back in the gardens of the Central Palace in the days of the Lord Leader Linn. And that he was being chased by the other children. In the nightmare, his one hope was that he would be able to control the sphere of energy before they could catch him.

The sphere, symbol of stupendous power, the almost godlike sphere—

Even in the dream he knew that both spheres, the one Czinczar had returned to him and the one they had taken from the little men, were far from the estate. And yet, as he ran in breathless terror, he tried to bring the sphere under his control. His mind seemed incapable of forming the cue thought.

The boys were closer. When he looked back, he could see their glittering eyes, their lips parted eagerly. Even their savage shouts floated out to him across the years, and echoed in his mind with all the old impact.

And then, just as their outstretched fingers snatched at him, just as utter despair seized on him, he spoke aloud the cue word for the sphere.

He woke up, perspiring with fear, but almost instantly he slept again. And once more the boys were after him. He realized, simply, that he had been wrong in trying to say the cue word. What he really wanted was to get to the black box that normally contained the sphere.

He reached it, and ecstatic with joy, started to climb into it. He knew—somehow he knew—if he crawled inside, the other boys would not notice him. He snuggled deep into the box—it was deeper than he remembered it—and he was sinking into a curious shadowless darkness when he thought sharply, *What am I doing here? Where is this leading me?*

For a long time, he pondered the implications. And then, very slowly and painfully, he pushed the covers aside. He sat up, nauseated but determined. *Sick or not,* he thought, *I'm getting up.*

He would go aboard the *Solar Star.* In the great chemical laboratories of the ship, he had during the long voyage found time to mix some of the drugs described in some old medical books he had found. He had tried them out first on the obviously dying, then cautiously on the sick. Some of them had been remarkably effective against respiratory diseases.

A nurse came into the room. He looked up at her blurrily. "My clothes," he mumbled, "bring my clothes."

"Your excellency," she stammered, "you mustn't. You're sick. You must get back into bed."

She didn't wait for a reply. She hurried out of the room. A minute later, the estate physician came running in. He rushed over to the bed, and Clane felt himself shoved irresistibly onto his back. The sheets were drawn up over his body.

He protested with a momentary fire. "Doctor, I want my clothes. I've got to go to the ship——" His voice faded to a mutter.

Above him, the blurred figure of the doctor turned to the blurred figure of the nurse. "Ship," he said. "What does he want to do? Get into a fight?"

There was a pause. Then the doctor spoke again, "Nurse, bring in the other women, and give him a cold bath. I think he needs a shock."

The water felt vaguely numb, as if it was not quite reaching him. He accepted the sensation passively, but he thought with a measure of sardonicism, *I'm caught here. I can't get away. They'll watch me night and day. They know all the petty cunnings of an invalid. And somehow at this eleventh hour my rank means nothing.*

He couldn't remember being carried back to bed, but suddenly he was under the sheets again. They felt heavier now, as if more weight had been added. He wondered if they were trying to hold him down by sheer load of blankets. Above him, one of the nurses said, "He's asleep. That's good. I think he'll be better when he wakes up."

He didn't feel as if he was sleeping. Nor was he exactly in a dream. He seemed to be standing on a green lawn, and

166

curiously Madelina was there beside him, smiling and saying, "I'll be good for you. You need somebody like me."

He remembered that with a faint smile. His smile faded, and he turned and said to Jerrin, "I'm afraid this means that Czinczar is the next Lord Leader. The Linns are going down. All the struggle was for nothing . . . nothing—"

Far away, somebody said, "The Patronate has been advised. A Council of Nine has been set up to govern the empire—"

He was alone on the green lawn, walking in the fresh air, breathing deeply. There was a forest ahead, with shadows under the trees. Figures flitted from bole to bole. He seemed to recognize them, and yet he couldn't decide who they were.

He came to the edge of the forest, hesitated; and then, aware of Madelina close behind him, walked on into the shadows.

He awakened, and opened his eyes.

It was as if vistas had sealed shut, fantastic depths receded behind him. He felt relaxed and at ease. His vision was clear, his body cool and comfortable. Clane turned his head.

Czinczar, haggard and hollow-cheeked, sat in a deep chair beside the bed. The sight of him shocked the beginning of memory in Clane. He remembered that drugs had been brought him from the ship.

He lay in bed, well but weak. And he said to Czinczar, "How long did it take?"

"Eighteen days."

The barbarian smiled wanly. "We had to fight our way in here," he said. "When I heard that you were dying, I sent an ultimatum to your doctor. When he didn't answer, I came down with three of your trained pharmacists, and an army. Since all your resonators were from the ship, and tuned to us, we just moved in."

He broke off. "How come you had such a stupid ignoramus around? After the medical work you did on the ship coming back here—"

Clane was apologetic. "I'd forgotten he was around here. I was so busy when we first came back. Besides, I was ill and lacking in sense."

A thought struck him. He stared at Czinczar with a

167

sharper appreciation of the implications of the barbarian's presence. Here was a leader schooled in bloodthirsty tactics. And yet he had come selflessly to help his chief rival for power in the solar system.

Czinczar seemed to realize what he was thinking. "Your excellency," he said grimly, "for eighteen days I have kept a vigil beside your bed because I have no better answer to the problem of the Riss than all the fools of Linn—out there." He gestured sweepingly with one hand. He went on, "It seems incredible, but the human race can only be saved by one man, and how *he* hopes to do it I cannot even imagine."

He paused. In a curious way, he looked so tense that Clane was electrified. The barbarian nodded bleakly. "You're guessing right," he said. "The Riss war is on. And already, all the old plans I had for resisting them are beginning to look like the stupidity of a diseased mind."

He broke off. "For six days," he said simply, "hundreds of Riss battleships have been attacking human settlements of every size. I couldn't even estimate for you what the losses have been. Men and women and children are dying in agony. Unquestionably this seems to be the second and last phase."

Once more his tone changed. "Your excellency," he said harshly, "we must wipe out these monsters to the last individual."

"No!" said Clane.

He sat up slowly, conscious of his weakness. But his eyes met the other's bloodshot gaze steadily.

"Czinczar," he said, "tomorrow morning we drop a picturized ultimatum giving the Riss a month to get out of the solar system, and to accept the sharing idea as a permanent policy."

"And if they refuse?" There was a sharp doubt in the barbarian's voice. He added a protest, "Your excellency, in one month, fifty million people will be—"

Clane went on as if he hadn't heard. "Beginning about two days from now, we start destroying their forces and their civilization everywhere. The exact time depends on how soon I can get up."

He shook his head savagely at Czinczar. "Don't get alarmed. I've never felt saner. I'm ready and in position at last. I tell you, my friend, I see things that no man or brain has ever seen before. All the preliminary tests have been made, although I've still got to take some special electronic photographs."

"And then what?"

"A part at least of the innermost meaning of matter and energy will be revealed."

XXVI

FOR A MINUTE after he entered, Clane was unobserved. He took the opportunity to look over his audience.

It was a distinguished assembly gathered there in the great physics laboratory aboard the magnificent—formerly Riss, now Linnan—warship, *Solar Star*. The Temple Scientists present looked bright and clean in their white dress robes. Government officials were amazingly well garbed; they were top men, of course, and would have control of available materials.

Of all the guests, the great nobles looked the shabbiest. Their estates had been virtually taken over by hordes of refugees, and it was the common practice during the crisis to maintain an appearance of equal suffering. For some reason, as Clane had observed during the barbarian invasion, this seemed to satisfy the landless, the moneyless and the witless about equally.

People were suddenly observing him. The babble of conversation died. Lord Clane hesitated a moment longer, and then walked through the cordon of soldiers who had been assigned to protect the line of machines from curious visitors. He switched on the power in the all-energy microscope, the all-energy camera, and the other instruments that would be brought into play. And then he turned to face the guests, the last of whom were settling into their chairs.

Clane motioned the porters to bring forward the sphere

and its container. When it had been set in its proper place under one of the glistening machines, he pressed a button. A television camera poked into the sphere as it rolled by, then moved backward and forward in perfect synchronization with it.

He flicked his hand over another switch; the lights went out. A huge screen glided down from the ceiling. On it appeared the stellar universe. Clane indicated the faintly glowing sphere to the right of the screen, rolling back and forth. "The scene you are gazing at is inside this," he said.

The idea must have been too new for them to grasp. Or perhaps they rejected his explanation even as he finished speaking. Nobody seemed surprised, which was not normal.

He waited till the stability of that blazing mass of stars had been established. And then, simply by thinking it so, started the entire mass into motion past the camera. At first the movement was not apparent. And then, a blazing sun swept toward them. It grew vast on the screen, and then swiftly began to slip by. A planet, tremendously nearby, touched the edge of the screen, and rolled in closer majestically. In the distance, a moon was visible. Clane identified them.

"Our earth and our moon," he said, "and that was our sun. Let's bring them into the room, shall we?"

He didn't expect them to understand that. He shut off the camera, waited till the screen was dead; and thought for an instant. There was a collective gasp from his audience. A blazing white ball about three inches in diameter flashed into view, and moved over under the microscope viewing lens. The room was abruptly as bright as day.

Clane said into the deathly stillness that followed the gasp, "Although it is hard to realize, this is our sun. Although it's impossible to see them with the naked eye, all the planets are with it. Mercury, Venus, Earth, Mars, Jupiter, and so on."

He waited, and a man said in a strained voice, "But how is that possible? We're sitting here in a ship a few miles *above* Earth."

Clane did not answer. For this was one of the basic secrets of the space-time-place continuum. The Riss had isolated a by-product in their "protector" device with its resonating energy flow, that intruded momentarily into every space-time field.

But here in the sphere and *its* by-products must be an answer closer to the final reality than any that had ever been dreamed of.

A rational cosmology? Surely, for the first time in the history of life, people were gazing into the deeps of the meaning of things. Which came first, thought of the Universe, or the Universe itself? The answer must be intricately interwoven into the very nature of things. Size, speed, space, *place*— all are in the understanding, not the reality. A dead man has no awareness of either. A living man can gaze a billion light-years into darkness at galaxies speeding off into still greater "distances." But he cannot easily adjust to the fourth dimensional understanding that will make it possible for him to comprehend the entire universe as a momentary thought in his own mind. It would have no size other than his own estimate, no speed except in relation to himself.

"And now"—Clane turned—"we have here an earth the size of a grain of dust. That's quite big. With an all-energy range microscope we can enlarge it hundreds of millions of times. That will give us a vast globe to look at, which we can only hope to see in small segments."

He was aware of scores of eyes watching him as he bent over the instrument. He made the necessary adjustments, then straightened, and said, "I've fitted the machine with an infra needle, which I can describe to you only by giving you some meaningless figures. The Riss used them to pierce objects of one-ten millionth of a millimeter. I shall use it as one might use a stabbing knife."

He paused to let the mystifying words sink in. Then he said, "Now, I bring our tiny sun and its planets into position, where the microscope can be concentrated on Earth."

He peered into the instrument's eyepiece. Without looking up, he said, "I can see Earth below. It does not appear to be spinning, and yet its speed of rotation must be about twelve thousand a second. That would be in proportion to its size. I haven't figured it out, because what I intend to do will depend on automatic machinery.

"The fact that thousands of twenty-four hour days seem to be passing every second is an appearance only. There is an unbreakable relationship between ourselves and that Earth. The timing will be exact."

He went on, "You may ask, how can I possibly hope to see anything on an object moving at that terrific speed of rotation. Especially since it's making thirty circuits of the sun every 'second.' My answer is that the Riss have supplied us with all the necessary automatic devices. It's a matter of synchronization, impossible for the human mind, but simple for energy circuits. I did a little practicing on the Moon yesterday just to make sure that the theory was sound."

He straightened, picked up a pile of photographs, and carried them to the nearest person. "Start them around," he said.

He ignored the oh-ing and ah-ing that started almost at once. Back in front of the towering microscope he picked up the thread of his explanation.

"Speed is of little or no account when these relays are in action. This Riss camera takes millions of pictures a second. The pictures are not photographed on film, but are stored in a tube. And the way they can be used goes something like this.

"Yesterday, as you may recall, we visited the mountain cities, and looked down on them, one after another, from a safe distance. What you don't know is that I took photographs of each one and stored them in the tube."

He had been peering into the eyepiece as he spoke. Now, once more he straightened. "At this moment, the camera is taking pictures of Earth every time it passes underneath. When I press home this lever, it will take pictures only of the area of that tiny globe which compares in structure to one of the photographs I took yesterday of a Riss-controlled city."

He pressed the lever.

A shield slid between the brilliant sun and the audience, effectively dimming the screen. There was an area of brightness on the screen.

"Ah, I see it's not quite in focus," said Clane.

He made another adjustment. The result showed immediately. The bright area on the screen cleared, and became a city in a mountain setting.

A bass voice said, "Why, that's Denra."

172

"I thought," said Clane, "I'd give us all a ringside seat for the show."

And still, he realized, from their faint reaction, they had no idea of what was coming. It was no wonder; he had to admit that. They were witnessing the co-ordination of Riss and human science at its highest level—and they simply didn't have the background to grasp the stupendousness of what was about to happen.

Inexorably, he went on, "The next step is to synchronize our stabbing 'needle.' Please realize, all of you, that when used against an earth the size of a dust mote, the thrust of a 'point' one ten-millionth of a millimeter in diameter could be disastrous. The instruments must be set, accordingly, to strike a surface blow only, like this—"

On the screen, the city of Denra dissolved in a cloud of dust. Part of a mountain was indented as by a colossal hammer to a depth of about a mile.

"The beauty of it," said Clane in an even, remorseless tone, "is that there is no radioactivity, and no counterattack possible. Now, obviously we're not going to destroy our own cities unless we have to, even though they are occupied by the Riss at the moment. I think we should give the invaders a chance to think over what has happened, while we switch to another city, this time not on Earth but on the Riss planet the *Solar Star* visited. I took the necessary photographs while we were there, because even then I was thinking along these lines."

It required about a minute to bring that sun and its planets out of the sphere and under the all-energy microscope.

Clane said, "As you know, our terms have been broadcast. We used a series of pictures to tell our story. We require surrender of half the battleships that came to the solar system, co-operation in our galactic peace program—which includes mutual development of all newly discovered habitable planets and a partial sharing of many worlds already inhabited. The interstellar television mechanism, transferred from the second ship we captured, is aboard and in operation—unfortunately, the second ship itself is still out of commission. So far we have received no reply to our ultimatum. It therefore becomes necessary to convince a stubborn enemy on part of his home territory that he must co-operate or die."

He touched a button, and the Riss city on the screen dissolved as if it were made of powder. The blow seemed harder than the first one, for not only was the city squashed but the great mountain beyond it ripped apart like a piece of cloth.

"I'm setting now for an even deeper thrust," said Clane. "The reason is that we 'photographed' Riss-controlled cities only on Earth and on the one Riss planet we visited. Any blows we deliver against other Riss planets marked on the captured star maps will have to be made in haphazard fashion, that is, without benefit of a preliminary 'photograph'. I think we can always hit a mountain area, but we must strike hard enough so that the effect is felt violently a hundred miles away—"

In spite of his will to calmness, his voice faltered. His audience was deathly silent, but the members could not possibly realize, as he did, the vast scope of what was happening. The Universe was tamed. Man need never again look out at the stars and feel small and insignificant. The grandeur of space-time remained as great as ever, but the veil was lifting. The days when the very mystery and size overwhelmed the wondering minds of those who gazed were not past. Yet surely it would never again be quite the same.

Clane covered his own feeling of awe by taking his time with the preliminaries to the next blow. Finally, feeling himself under control again, he said, "I imagine it will take time for them to accept the bitter reality of their defeat. We'll just have to keep on punishing them till they signal us that they are prepared to discuss terms."

Four hours went by before that signal came.

A year had passed. As he walked beside Czinczar, Clane said, "It still looks ugly to me."

The two of them, Clane in a drab priestly gown and Czinczar wearing the uniform of a private in the barbarian army—a common sight around Linn these days—walked slowly up to the newly finished victory column.

Clane studied it. It stood in the great square before the Central Palace. Its construction had been voted by the Patronate, and it consisted of an enormous cube of marble on top of which an intricate scene was arranged. A man in the gown of a temple scientist stood astride two planets. High above his head, he held a third planet in his hands. He stood on his tiptoes as if reaching for something. All around his feet were other planets and some star-shaped objects.

The gown, unlike anything Clane had ever worn, was a bright gold in color. It gleamed in the afternoon sun.

The figure bore a rather striking facial resemblance to Clane, but the body was huge out of proportion to the rest of the statuary. A giant towered there.

Clane turned to speak to Czinczar, and saw that the other was watching a couple that had paused a few feet away.

"Look at that," said the man to the woman. " 'Savior of the race', it says there. What will these ruling families think of next?"

The woman said, "Are you sure it's a member of the ruling family? Oh, there's the name up there." She moved her lips as if she were reading it to herself. Then she said, "Clane Linn. Which one is that?" They drifted off in the direction of the palace.

Clane said dryly, "Such is fame."

He saw that Czinczar was smiling. The great man was smiling. "It's a big world," he said. "Why should they know your name, or what you look like? They didn't see you do anything. Perhaps when we get a wider distribution of television, you may be recognized on every street corner."

Clane said, "I'm not arguing with you. How much thought do I give to the great men of the past? I'll divide that by ten, and assume my proper position in the hall of fame." He added, "It's good that men forget their heros and their gods. If they didn't, life would be drab indeed for the newborn."

Czinczar said, "I'm sorry I couldn't get here in time for the unveiling. Let's sit down for a minute."

He motioned Clane to one of the hard stone benches. Presently a group of laughing girls came by. They did not even glance at the column, or at the two men who sat beneath it.

Two young men carrying artists' palettes and easels, unfolded their equipment and sat down on benches across the walk from the work. They began to paint.

"What I like about it," said one, "is the way it silhouettes against the sky. If I can blur it in properly in the foreground, I think I can make a wonderful cloud scene."

"It's an atrocious work of art," said the other, "but statuary pictures have a fairly steady sale. When a new one comes along, the important thing is to get at it first. If I can place a dozen copies in the best shops, I'll have orders for hundreds of them."

They fell silent again. After several minutes, the second man came over to Clane and Czinczar. "I'm trying to draw this statue," he said, "and you two men add nothing to the scene sitting on that bench. If you don't mind, I'd like both of you to stand up and raise your right hands as if you're paying tribute to a hero. I assure you I won't take very long. I'm a fast worker, and I can sketch your likenesses in a few minutes."

He must have misread Clane's expression, for he shrugged, and said, "If you don't care to do that, I wonder if you would mind moving over to those other benches."

Czinczar glanced ironically at the Lord Leader of Linn, then he stood up. He said, "I question if my friend should pose in front of this particular statue, but I shall be very happy to do so in the position you suggested."

"Thank you," said the artist.

He went back to his easel.